HERE COMES MY EARL

ANNA BRADLEY

OLIVER-HEBER BOOKS

CHAPTER
ONE
HYDE PARK, LONDON, EARLY SPRING, 1817

A sage had once said there was nothing new under the sun.

Or they'd said something to that effect, at any rate. Phee couldn't recall the precise words, but the sage had claimed there wasn't a single thing to be seen or heard that hadn't been seen and heard before, and then they'd gone on to lament the wearisome nature of human existence.

The name of this grim prophet escaped her now, but there was only one thing that could have led to such gloomy reflections.

The London season. What else?

Nothing— *nothing* —could be more tedious, more wearisome, more apt to elicit such hopeless melancholy than the London season. Of all the things under the sun guilty of tiresome monotony, the London season was the guiltiest, and nowhere was that more evident than Hyde Park during the fashionable hour.

An entire year had passed since she'd last ventured here, yet aside from a few new faces, these were all the same people who'd appeared on the promenade last season, and all of them as eager as ever to be seen in their sleek carriages, or mincing along the promenade in their most fashionable clothing.

The costumes were different this time. If she could judge by the ladies' walking dresses, this season's color appeared to be celestial blue, as opposed to last season's fawn— but not the mincing.

That never changed. The *ton* remained as pleased with themselves as they'd always been, and as eager to parade about showing off their finery.

"My goodness, Euphemia." Lady Fosberry nudged her. "Do stop grimacing, won't you? You look as if you've been stuck with a hatpin."

"Grimacing? Whatever do you mean? I'm *smiling*, my lady." Why, anyone could see she was utterly delighted to be here. *Delighted*, dash it. There wasn't a single thing she'd rather be doing than riding in endless circles around the Ring during the fashionable hour.

She shrank back against the squabs, but short of throwing herself down upon the floorboards, there was no way to avoid the disapproving gazes of the *ton*. It wasn't like a ball, where a lady could duck into an alcove or retreat to the ladies' retiring room when her skin began to prickle from the weight of all the prying eyes on her.

Here, there was no place to hide.

"Would we call that a smile?" Lady Fosberry studied her, then shook her head. "No, I think not. Come now, Euphemia. Lady Ellsworth's carriage is approaching, and we don't wish to give her any reason to gossip about you."

Ah. That, right there, was proof of her theory. Lady Ellsworth had been a spiteful gossip last season, and the season before that, and now here she was again, as much a spiteful gossip as she'd ever been. "Nothing good ever came of attracting Lady Ellsworth's attention."

"No, but you can't escape such unpleasantness entirely, my dear. Life is a messy business. The best you can do is take your chances, and face it when it comes."

"How reassuring you are, my lady." Still, Phee did as she was told, and stretched her lips into a smile. Not that it would do any good. She might smile all she liked, and Lady Ellsworth would still pour an endless stream of vicious gossip about her into every willing ear in London.

"It may be someone's smile, but it isn't *yours*, Euphemia. Not your real one." Lady Fosberry frowned. "This one's a trifle maniacal."

Behind her frozen lips, Phee gritted her teeth. "Why shouldn't I be smiling? It's a lovely day."

"It is, indeed. One couldn't ask for a prettier one. It's such a shame Harriett and James didn't arrive in time to accompany us this afternoon." Lady Fosberry let out a heavy sigh. "They were meant to arrive before tea time. I can't imagine what's keeping them."

"I'm sure they'll be along soon, my lady."

"Yes, I suppose so. Good afternoon, Lady Ellsworth!" Lady Fosberry waved as Lady Ellsworth passed them in her smart peacock blue carriage with the shiny black trim, the gold buttons of her driver's livery glinting in the sun.

"Lady Fosberry." Lady Ellsworth tipped her head in gracious acknowledgment of the greeting, but she only spared a cool nod for Phee, who smiled so hard in return that her cheeks ached.

All these contortions couldn't be good for her

complexion. Already cracks were threatening to appear at the corners of her lips, and she'd only just arrived in London. At this rate, by mid-season, they'd have spread like furrows in a patch of parched earth. Soon enough her skin would flake away entirely, and bits and pieces of her would whirl away in the chill wind, never to be seen again.

How delighted the *ton* would be then! She could hear the whispers now.

Did you hear, my dear? Euphemia Templeton disintegrated into dust in the middle of the Ring, and during the fashionable hour, no less! One moment she was there, and then *poof*! She blew away, right in front of poor Lady Ellsworth! Terribly vulgar, but that's just like the Templetons, isn't it? They're never happy unless they're causing a scandal.

It wasn't true, about the scandals. A lady would have to be daft to wish to catch the judgmental eyes of the *ton*. Right now, for instance, there were dozens of other fashionable people in the Ring, all of them far more interesting than she was, but the *ton* was so preoccupied with gawking at her, they hardly spared anyone else a glance.

Alas, there was nothing to be done about it. It wasn't as if she'd expected anonymity after last season's dreadful debacle, and it would only become worse once Lady Fosberry's niece Harriett arrived.

Thank goodness she'd managed to talk Tilly and Kit out of remaining in London for the season! After much cajoling on her part, she'd at last persuaded them to go to Oxfordshire to await the impending birth of Juliet's first child. She missed them horribly, but the last thing this season needed was another Templeton sister for the *ton* to fixate on.

"I don't mind telling you, Euphemia, that I'm a trifle worried about Harriett's season," Lady Fosberry murmured. "The *ton* has a long memory for scandal."

"I know, my lady. I'm worried, as well." Phee gave her ladyship's hand a reassuring squeeze, but all the reassurance in the world didn't change the fact that Harriett's circumstances were decidedly precarious.

Last season had been Harriett's first foray into London's marriage mart. It should have been her last, but things had gone so drastically, so spectacularly wrong that poor Harriett's season had ended with near ruination, instead of a betrothal.

If such a thing happened again this season— indeed, if Harriett set so much as a toe out of line —the *ton* would finish her.

"I do hope James hasn't changed his mind about Harriett's having a second season." Lady Fosberry ducked closer, hiding her face under the edge of her new beaver fur hat, and setting the large feather fixed to the brim quivering. "He threatened at one point to keep her in Hereford. He put up rather a fuss about it, but I insisted we can't hide Harriett away in the country as if she's done something wrong."

"Of course not!" Why, of all the young ladies in the world, Harriett was the last one who deserved such a fate. It would be wrong of her brother to treat her as if she'd done something to be ashamed of, or as if she were a disgrace to the family name. "Surely, he wouldn't do such a thing?"

"I don't think so, no." But despite her denial, Lady Fosberry was worrying at the rug they'd tucked over their knees, twisting it between her fingers. "He only wants to keep her safe, you know. In the end, he seemed to agree that she must have another season, but perhaps he's changed his mind. One can never tell with James."

On the contrary, one could tell a great deal about Lord Fairmont, and on quite a short acquaintance, at that, but Phee kept that opinion locked tight behind the rigid smile on her lips.

If she *were* to say something, however, she might just *hint* to Lady Fosberry that Lord Fairmont seemed to her to be the sort of gentleman who had very decided opinions about matters he knew little about.

Denying Harriett a second season would almost certainly condemn her to a lifetime of loneliness. "Does Lord Fairmont not wish for his sister to marry?"

"He does, indeed." Lady Fosberry continued to pick at the rug, her face clouded. "So much so, he's chosen a gentleman for her."

"*He's* chosen?" Goodness, he was determined to protect Harriett from the *ton*'s wagging tongues, wasn't he? Then again, she didn't know why she was so surprised at it. It wasn't unusual for a brother to choose his sister's spouse. "Given Harriett's circumstances, it might be the wisest course of action, as long as she approves his choice."

"She doesn't," Lady Fosberry said shortly. "Not at all."

"Oh, dear. Who did he choose for her?"

Lady Fosberry had been staring down at the rug in her lap, but now she pushed it aside and turned to face Phee. "It's rather bad, I'm afraid."

"Who? Not Lord Bourke, I hope?" Poor Lord Bourke was as dull as a Sunday sermon, which might have been forgivable, if he hadn't also been as condescending as one. "Or... oh, no! It's not Lord Winchell, is it?" Lord Winchell had the temperament of a secondary school headmaster, and alas, also the face of one.

Lady Fosberry shook her head. "No, it's neither of them. I'm afraid it's worse than that."

Worse than Lord Winchell? Dear God. "Who? Who is it?"

Lady Fosberry closed her eyes. "The Earl of Farthingale."

"Farthingale!" Phee stared at Lady Fosberry, horrified. "But he won't do at all! He's much too old for Harriett!"

"He's not, actually. He's only twenty-eight."

"No, that can't be right. It's impossible!" Why, the man was forty years old if he was a day.

"Indeed, it isn't. He and James were at Oxford together."

Phee fell back against the squabs, aghast. Of all the gentlemen Lord Fairmont might have chosen for Harriett, Lord Farthingale was the worst of the lot.

Although... well, it must be said that from a strictly practical point of view, Harriett and Lord Farthingale weren't an entirely unlikely match. They came from similar backgrounds, both of them having been born and raised in Herefordshire, and in similar circumstances.

There wasn't a thing in Lord Farthingale's background to give an overprotective brother a moment's concern. He was a wealthy earl and a man of impeccable reputation. In a logical, mathematical sense, they were well suited. If she hadn't known Harriett as well as she did, she might even have matched her with Lord Farthingale herself.

The trouble was, the *reality* of Lord Farthingale

was a different matter entirely than the *idea* of Lord Farthingale. On paper, they weren't a bad match, but from a *human* standpoint, there weren't two people in the world more ill-suited to each other than Harriett and Lord Farthingale.

How ironic, that *she*, of all people, should be arguing against a logical match! Perhaps there were still a few new things to be found under the sun, after all.

There'd been a time before each of her sisters had fallen in love when she'd insisted on the superiority of a logical, mathematically sound match. It was how this ill-fated matchmaking business had begun.

But now... well, a lady who'd witnessed each of her four younger sisters fall madly in love with the most unlikely gentlemen, and go on to make four implausible matches with said gentlemen, all of whom loved them madly in return— how could such a lady continue to believe that love wasn't the key to matrimonial happiness?

Love did exist, as it turned out, and there were those who were able to take the love they'd found and turn it into happiness.

Not everyone, though. For her, love had been fleeting. It hadn't even outlasted her first London season.

Six years had rolled by since then.

Six years.

It seemed like an insignificant amount of time when one thought of it, and sounded like it if one said it aloud, but for her, six years had been a lifetime.

Long enough to transform a girl into a young woman, and a young woman into a spinster.

It was certainly enough time for a silly, starry-eyed young lady's every cherished hope to disappear like a wisp of smoke into a cloudless sky.

Gone, in the blink of an eye.

She couldn't stand back and watch the same thing happen to Harriett. Anyone could see at a single glance that a match between Harriett and Lord Farthingale was out of the question. It would only lead to misery.

Harriett was tenderhearted kindness, sweetness, and light, whereas Lord Farthingale...

Was *not*. He was a gentleman of stern countenance and rigid principles— a grim, dark-tempered man who was apt to find fault with everyone and everything around him. Seeing Harriett sacrificed to such a man would be like watching a thick, dark storm cloud eclipse the sun.

What in God's name could Lord Fairmont be *thinking*?

"You can imagine Harriett's reaction to James's choice." Lady Fosberry heaved a sigh. "She flatly refused to even entertain the possibility of a match with Lord Farthingale. I'm afraid poor James was rather astonished by her vehemence. It's caused quite a row between them."

"He wouldn't force her into the marriage, would he?" Goodness, what a dreadful thought.

"No. He cares too much for her to wish to see her unhappy, but James can be terribly stubborn about such things. Nearly as stubborn as Harriett. So, my dearest Euphemia, as you can see, we're at quite an impasse. It won't be an easy season, I'm afraid."

"I don't think there is such a thing, my lady."

"No, perhaps not. There's one other thing you should know, as well. Harriett is... how can I put this delicately? She hasn't said as much to me, but I have reason to believe she's enamored of another gentleman."

"But that's wonderful!" She'd feared Harriett might shy away from risking her heart again after the fiasco with Lord Wyle, but then Harriett was a much more resilient young lady than her delicate appearance would suggest. "I should think that would solve all our problems."

If Harriett was in love with another gentleman, then surely, that was the end of it. Lord Fairmont couldn't be so cruel as to keep her from the gentleman she loved.

"It will, if the gentleman in question can earn Lord Fairmont's approval."

"Surely, that won't be a problem?"

"Er, well, I'm afraid there may be one or two tiny... that is, he's not quite—"

"Lady Fosberry! Halloo, Lady Fosberry!"

"What in the world?" Lady Fosberry turned at the shout, startled. It wasn't at all the thing to bellow a lady's name whilst parading around the Ring, particularly with so many high-strung horses about.

"My goodness! Who's that?" Phee turned toward the voice, rising a little from her seat so she might see where the shout was coming from, but it seemed as if every member of the *ton* was crowded into the Ring, and the small space was choked with carriages. "I can't see a blessed thing."

"Lady Fosberry! Over here! How do you do, my lady?"

The crowd parted then, and one would-be whip — a young, ginger-haired gentleman in a canary yellow coat came charging through the gap, one hand on the ribbons, and the other waving his hat over his head.

"Oh, dear." Lady Fosberry's face drained of color as he careened toward them. "My dear Lord Gilbert, please do take care!" she cried, trying to wave him down.

But it was all in vain. The gentleman continued to tear recklessly along in his apple green, high perch phaeton, as if utterly unaware of the impropriety of rushing about willy-nilly in the close confines of the Ring.

One went in a circle, period. One did not charge through the center, kicking dust about and frightening the other horses, but this gentleman behaved as if his was the only carriage there, seemingly unaware of the dirt flying out from behind his bright red wheels, and without any thought for the equipages behind him, or the disgruntled drivers shaking their fists in his wake.

"Dear God!" Phee gasped as he tore past a terrified pony pulling a pair of scandalized ladies in a low phaeton. "He'll overset his carriage, and break his fool of a neck!"

"His, or someone else's!" Lady Fosberry echoed.

Just then, the gentleman, who seemed to have at last realized the chaos he was causing, jerked his phaeton to the left in an attempt to stop, but he miscalculated the turn, and came up hard against the low railing surrounding the Ring.

A screech rent the air and the half-dozen young ladies who'd been strolling down the adjacent pathway scattered like a flock of birds.

"What can he be thinking, driving so danger-

11

ously? Lyman, can't you do something?" Lady Fosberry turned to her driver in alarm.

By then, Lyman was already attempting to move out of the way, but there was no place for him to go. The Ring was so choked with carriages he had no room to shift away. All he could do was maneuver their carriage so if the phaeton struck them, it would hit the back of the equipage, rather than the side. "Hang on, ladies!"

"Lord Gilbert, my dear boy, just stay where you are!" Lady Fosberry held her hands out in front of her, but alas, Lord Gilbert had lost all control over his horses. Their eyes rolled in their heads as they broke away from the railing with such force he was thrown backward in his seat.

There was no chance of his regaining control of them— no stopping the inevitable collision. "Quickly, my lady." Phee braced herself against Lady Fosberry, and with all her might, began shoving her toward the carriage door. If they could make it over the fence before the phaeton struck, they'd be safe.

"I can't— no, Euphemia! I can't—"

"Yes, you can!" With a strength born of panic, she wrenched Lady Fosberry out of her seat, and somehow between coaxing, pushing, and shoving, she got her halfway over the side of the carriage door. "There, now over the fence— no, don't look down! Yes, that's it, my lady!"

Lady Fosberry let out a terrified shriek, but she managed to scramble over the fence, and an instant later she dropped down onto the dirt pathway on the other side.

Oh, thank goodness!

Phee crawled across the seat, ready to hurl herself

out of the carriage after Lady Fosberry, but just as she'd clambered to her knees, one of the runaway horses broke loose. Beneath her, the carriage gave a heart-stopping lurch. The entire frame shuddered around her, tossing her backward against the seat.

The horse attempted to bolt, but his reins were hopelessly tangled with the others. He was trapped, and in an increasing panic, he lurched into the gap between the carriage and the fence, his hooves clawing the air, cutting off her only route to safety. If she attempted to escape from the other door, she'd almost certainly be trampled.

It was too late to move, too late to jump, too late to even catch her breath.

There was no place for her to go, nothing for her to do but retreat to the far side of the carriage, squeeze her eyes shut, and brace for what was to come.

TWO

H arriett was furious with him, and she wasn't taking any pains to hide it.

"Come now, Harriett. You've hardly said a word to me since we left Hereford. You keep insisting that you're old enough to make your own decisions, but you're behaving like a child having a tantrum." Then again, not many children had the fortitude to maintain an icy silence for three days running.

"There doesn't seem much point in speaking when no one is listening to me."

She lifted one shoulder in a shrug, but a telltale sniff and the wobbling of her chin gave her away. She was a breath away from a fresh bout of tears, and once they started to fall... well, it would be all over for him.

He couldn't bear to see Harriett cry. Even as a boy, he'd gone to ridiculous lengths to stop her tears and look where that had landed him. The powerful, wealthy Earl of Fairmont, brought low by the little bit of a sister whose curls he'd once brushed every morning, and whose shoes he'd once tied.

"I *have* been listening to you." The trouble wasn't a lack of attention on his part. If only it was so simple. But alas, attempting to reason with a young lady who'd taken an intense, and inexplicable dislike to a perfectly unobjectionable suitor was a great deal more complicated than that.

"I do beg your pardon, James, but if you'd been listening to me, we wouldn't be meeting Lord Farthingale this afternoon, and yet here we are." She waved a hand at their surroundings. "Nothing indicates an impending courtship quite as clearly as appearing together in Hyde Park during the fashionable hour."

"It's a ride around the Serpentine, Harriett, not a betrothal." There was no sign of Farthingale, at any rate. He'd been meant to meet them at the Columbia Gate, and he was nowhere to be seen. Perhaps Harriett succeeded in frightening him off when he'd come to visit them in Hereford.

It was nearing the end of the fashionable hour, but a glance ahead revealed only a pair of ladies in a sleek phaeton coming their way. They began whispering as soon as they caught sight of Harriett, and she quickly averted her gaze from their curious faces.

Damn it. He'd hoped to spare her this very thing. A betrothal to Farthingale would have made a second season unnecessary, but now Harriett was at the mercy of the smirking *ton*.

Harriett said nothing, but only let out a sigh as they passed through the Columbia Gate and turned onto North Carriage Drive. Neither of them spoke as they continued through the park toward the Serpentine, where they could glimpse the pale rays of spring sunlight glittering on the water.

Good Lord, this silence between them was torture.

Yet it continued to stretch on as they made the turn onto West Carriage Drive, until at last Harriett turned to face him, the tears he'd been dreading all afternoon sparkling in the corners of her eyes. "It's not a betrothal yet, no, but soon enough he'll be calling on me every afternoon, and before I know it you'll have foisted me off on a man I can never love, and my life will be ruined!"

Good Lord, more dramatics. How he despised them. "I don't intend to foist you off on any—"

"I never imagined my brother could be so cruel. How can you doom me to a life without love, James?"

Her voice rose with every word, and heads began to turn in their direction. Lady Arundel and Lady Silvester were coming toward them, their ponies' ears pricking at Harriett's exclamation as they drew near. They'd overheard her outburst, and he clicked his tongue at Nyx and Hemera, hurrying the horses toward a less crowded section of West Gate Drive, where they were safe from the gossips' prying ears.

"I have no intention of marrying you to a gentleman you don't love. How can you think I would? I've only ever wanted your happiness, Hattie."

"So you say, but if that's true, James, then why do you continue to insist upon forcing me into Lord Farthingale's company? He isn't the sort of gentleman who can ever make me happy."

"What's wrong with Farthingale? He's a perfectly respectable gentleman." Not an exciting one, no— one couldn't accuse Farthingale of being romantic or dashing —but surely that was a good thing? He wasn't going to marry his precious sister to one of the foolish, preening peacocks that passed for fashionable gentlemen these days.

Farthingale would make Harriett a solid, dependable husband.

"He's *old*, James. Close to forty, at least."

"Forty!" Farthingale was the same age as *he* was, damn it. "He's twenty-eight, Harriet. Hardly in his dotage."

"Is that all? He seems a great deal older than that. It must be those tight lines around his mouth." She laid her hand on his arm, her gaze pleading. "I know I made a dreadful mistake with Lord... a dreadful mistake last season, but does that mean I no longer deserve to be happy?"

"Of course not, Hattie. This has nothing to do with him."

Harriett never said the name of the man who'd come so close to ruining her, but the scoundrel was right here between them as surely as if he were perched on Harriet's lap.

Lord Wyle, the man who'd caused such strife between them.

Fortunately, Wyle had taken to his heels as soon as his perfidy was discovered, and run off to the Continent like the coward he was, saving James the effort of burying a ball in his skull.

But it hadn't ended there. The sordid business with Wyle marked the beginning of the first of a series of disagreements between himself and his sweet younger sister— the sister who'd never spoken a cross word to him in her life until Wyle had appeared and destroyed all her peace.

Despite what she believed, he'd never blamed Harriett for her catastrophic first season. She was young and naïve, and Wyle had taken great pains to hide his true nature from her. No, he put the blame where it belonged. On Wyle, for turning the head of a naive young lady. In his worst moments, he even blamed his Aunt Fosberry, who hadn't seen Harriett's danger until it was too late.

But most of all, he blamed himself, for the whole ugly, sordid mess. If he'd only returned from the Continent before the start of Harriett's season, Wyle never would have wormed his way into her affections, and she'd be safely wed to a proper gentleman by now.

A gentleman like Lord Farthingale, for instance. "I don't understand why you're so set against Farthingale, Harriett. If you'd only give him a chance, you'd see for yourself what an, er... steadfast, loyal, and faithful gentleman he is."

Loyal? Faithful? Good Lord, was that the best he could do? He'd made poor Farthingale sound like a Saint Bernard.

No young lady wanted to marry a Saint Bernard, for God's sake.

Harriett let out a heavy sigh. "I don't have anything against Lord Farthingale, James. I simply don't want to *marry* him."

"But how can you be so sure? You hardly know the man. You certainly don't know him well enough yet to have made up your mind not to marry him. I only ask that you give him a chance, Harriett."

"A lady knows these things, James."

"How?" How could she possibly know? She'd hardly exchanged a dozen words with Farthingale.

"I can't explain it to you. I simply *know*, that's all. Aunt Fosberry doesn't think Lord Farthingale is a proper match for me. She says he's too old, and too staid to make me happy."

Despite his every effort to remain calm, James's fingers tightened on the reins. His aunt would do well to keep out of this business. After all, she had approved of Wyle, and look how that had turned out. The man had tried to kidnap Harriett, and drag her off to Gretna Green!

"I daresay Phee won't like the match either," Harriett went on. "I trust her opinion. You'd do well to listen to her, James. She is London's most celebrated matchmaker."

James's teeth snapped together. If only he had a shilling for every time Harriett had said that woman's name to him.

Phee, or Miss Euphemia Templeton.

London's most celebrated matchmaker, indeed. It was absurd. If Euphemia Templeton was anything, it was London's most infamous troublemaker.

If there was one person he blamed more than himself for Harriett's disastrous season, it was Euphemia Templeton. She'd been the one to suggest the match with Lord Wyle in the first place. Considering what a disaster *that* had turned out to be, one would think she'd be ashamed to show her face again, but here she was in London, and as meddlesome as ever, filling Harriett's ears with her ridiculous opinions.

"Phee is ever so clever. She's never wrong about such things."

"She was wrong about Wyle, wasn't she?"

As soon as Wyle's name left his lips, he wanted to bite his tongue off. God above, why had he mentioned that scoundrel? He'd promised himself he'd never breathe a word of reproach regarding that business, but just the mention of Euphemia Templeton's name was enough to upset all his best intentions.

Something would have to be done about her, and soon, but not now. Not when Harriett's chin was wobbling again. "I beg your pardon, Harriett. I didn't mean to hurt your feelings."

"I know." She nodded, but she kept her face turned away from his, and she'd caught her lower lip between her teeth in the way she always did when she was trying not to cry. "It's alright."

But it wasn't alright. It hadn't been for some time now, and he cursed himself under his breath as another strained silence unfolded between them. It was becoming a common occurrence, these awkward silences.

He no longer knew what to say to her, or how to comfort her. He'd been a fool to think he could return after six years, and find his life just as he'd left it, as if no time had passed. Instead, he was like a misshapen puzzle piece, too warped to slip back into the place he'd once fit.

On the worst days, he felt as if he didn't even know Harriett anymore.

He cleared his throat, desperate to dispel the silence. "It's a lovely day, is it not? Very warm for spring."

The weather. He was talking to his beloved sister — the sister with whom he'd shared every secret, and who'd once told him all her childish dreams —he was talking to her about the *weather*, for God's sake.

Things had come to a sad pass, indeed.

"Yes, quite warm. I do hope we'll have a—"

A shriek echoed through the crisp, clear air, cutting Harriett off, and she turned to him, her eyes wide. "My goodness! What was that?"

Before he could reply, there was a second shriek, this one louder, and edged with terror. A man's shout followed, and the riders in front of them quickened their pace, eager to see what mayhem was on offer.

"Oh, dear. There's some sort of commotion." Harriett shaded her eyes, squinting at the small copse of elm trees ahead. "It looks as if there's a crowd gathering near the Ring."

"There's always a crowd near the Ring." The *ton* loved nothing more than making a spectacle of themselves, and there was no better place to show off their fine horses and carriages than the Ring.

It was impossible to see a thing from here, but as they drew closer to the Guard House he saw that Harriett was right. There was a growing knot of people converging near the Ring, some of them spilling onto the adjacent footpath. Several gentlemen had dismounted from their horses and were gesticulating wildly, their shouts growing in urgency as they pointed toward some disturbance unfolding in the Ring.

A carriage accident, perhaps? It wouldn't be the first time there'd been a collision, as the Ring was always crowded with carriages, and the *ton* on the whole were often too preoccupied with parading to pay proper attention to where they were going.

He clucked to Nyx and Hemera, who broke into a trot

"What's happening?" Harriett asked. "I can't see anything."

"No, not with all these people in the way." All he could see was a flash of bright yellow— a gentleman's coat? But the shrieking hadn't ceased, and from the earsplitting volume, this was no ordinary disturbance.

Those were screams of true terror.

"James!" Harriett grabbed his arm, her fingers digging into his coat sleeve. "Something's terribly wrong!"

"Take the reins, Hattie." He tossed them to her, then leaped down from his phaeton and set off for the footpath that skirted the eastern edge of the Serpentine, toward the Ring.

It wasn't until he reached the railing that separated the Ring from the footpath that he recognized his aunt's carriage, and it was... Good God, what was happening?

Her carriage was pushed hard against the railing, and trapped in place by a green, high-perch phaeton. A red-faced gentleman in a yellow coat was atop the box, tugging on the reins in a fruitless attempt to control his pair.

All was confusion, but it looked as if the gentleman in the yellow coat had lost control of his pair of high steppers. They'd bolted and were careening around the Ring in a panic, searching for a way out.

But there was no way out. The Ring was far too crowded, and somehow, the phaeton's ribbons had become snarled with his aunt's carriage ribbons. Her driver, Lyman, was making a heroic attempt to untangle them, but even from this distance James could see it was hopeless. The knots only pulled tighter as the high-steppers lunged this way and that, mindless with panic.

It was only a matter of time before they threw their driver from the box and bolted again, either dragging the carriage with them or crashing directly into it. "That fool is going to kill someone!"

Where was his aunt? Her driver, Lyman was still struggling with the ribbons and shouting something at the gentleman in the yellow coat, but he couldn't find his aunt. Had she fallen from the carriage? Damn it, he couldn't see a bloody thing! The entire Ring had descended into chaos, with everyone shouting at once, and—

Wait, just there!

Relief rushed through him as he caught sight of her on the other side of the railing. Somehow, she'd escaped her carriage and was safely out of the fray, but she continued to shriek as if she feared for her life, her panicked wails rising above the din.

She'd entirely lost her composure, and he soon saw why.

Miss Templeton was still in the carriage.

He hadn't noticed her at first, because she wasn't shrieking, or struggling, or gesticulating. She'd tucked herself into a corner of the carriage, as far from the horses as she could get. She had one hand braced on the seat beside her, and the other curled around the door. Her knuckles were white, and her face as pale as death, but despite being in more danger than anyone else in the Ring, she was utterly still and silent.

Behind him, Harriett shouted something, but there was no time to answer her— no time to do anything but jump over the railing and run for the trapped carriage. A tight circle had formed around the scene, all the gentlemen shouting instructions at once, but for all that they had endless ideas about how to correct the problem, none of them seemed at all eager to actually help, and he was obliged to shove them aside.

"Out of my way, damn you!"

He shoved his way past the heaving bodies, dodging carriages and treading on ladies' skirts as he tore across the Ring. He'd half hoped he might be able to calm the panicked horses, but it was already too late for that.

His only option was to get Miss Templeton out of the carriage before the entire thing toppled over and get her to the other side of the railing before either of them was trampled.

"Miss Templeton!" He darted past the struggling horses and came abreast of the carriage, but there was no way to reach the outside door without catching a hoof to the forehead, and the other door was pressed hard against the fencing, and trapped shut.

There was no help for it. She'd have to slide across the seat toward the fencing, scurry over the top edge of the carriage, and drop down on the other side.

With one leap, he scaled the fence, and leaned over the top railing, holding his arms out to her. "Quickly, Miss Templeton! Slide over to me, and I'll help you over the side!"

Her face went another shade whiter. "N-no, I can't! I can't—"

"Yes, you can. I'll help you, I promise it."

She squeezed her eyes closed, but just when he was certain he'd have to jump into the carriage himself and drag her out, she began to make her way across the seat.

"Yes, that's it. Good! Just a little further, and I'll be able to reach you."

It seemed to take hours, but she slid closer, inch by torturous inch until at last he could reach her. He grasped her forearm, and with one hard jerk, he tugged her the rest of the way across, so she was flush against the door. "Good! Now rise to your knees. Quickly, now. There's no time to waste."

The carriage was shuddering and swaying underneath them, and her body was shaking so hard it was a wonder she could move at all. Another lady might have swooned under such circumstances, but Miss Templeton set her jaw and did as he bid her.

As soon as she was on her knees, he caught her around the waist. "There. Very good, Miss Templeton. Now put your arms around my neck, and hold on as tightly as you can."

She wrapped her arms around his neck, her slender body trembling against him. He wrapped his other arm around her and spread his hand over the back of her head to protect it, then, with a quick shout to Lyman to abandon the carriage, he hauled her over the side of the door, and into his arms, pausing only to tuck her tightly against his chest before he sucked in a quick breath, and leaped over the fence.

They hit the ground with a bone-rattling thud, and an instant later, Lyman landed beside them with an "Oof!"

"Euphemia!" His aunt was upon them at once, falling to her knees beside them in the dirt. "Euphemia, can you hear me?"

"Miss Templeton?" Somehow, despite his best efforts, he'd landed on top of her. She lay unmoving beneath him, and he jerked up onto his elbows. "Miss Templeton! Are you alright?"

She didn't answer, and his heart rushed into his throat as he gazed down at her white face. Her eyes were closed, and there was a streak of dirt on her temple.

Dear God, had he crushed her? Broken one of her ribs, or—

Her eyelids fluttered open, and for a single instant, an instant only, their gazes locked, and they looked deeply into each other's eyes.

And for that instant, that single instant only, everything around him faded to silence until only one thought remained in his head.

Blue. Her eyes were blue.

CHAPTER
THREE

"Euphemia! Why isn't she waking up, James? She looks very bad, indeed!"

It was Lady Fosberry's voice, but the face that swam into focus as Phee's vision began to clear *didn't* belong to her ladyship. It was a familiar face, with noble cheekbones, and a strong, angular jaw. She'd seen it before, but she couldn't quite remember—

"Phee! Are you alright? What a dreadful tumble!"

That was certainly Harriett speaking, but her voice was higher than usual— rather a squeak, really —as if she were distressed about something.

But what? What had happened?

Was she alright? She hadn't the faintest idea, but one thing was certain.

She wasn't as she should be.

Her lungs were moving in great, heaving pants, but for all her gasping, her breath was trapped deep inside her chest, under her breastbone, and she was lying atop something hard and... gritty?

Then there was the matter of the face above hers.

It was a gentleman's face, with a forbidding, grim line of a mouth.

That mouth... she'd seen it before. Studied it, even, and wondered about how his lips might look if he ever smiled, but she'd never seen such a thing as a smile there. No, neither quirk nor curve had ever graced those handsome lips.

It was a pity. He had such a pleasing mouth. A smile would do wonders for his—

"For pity's sake, James, do get up! The poor child can't breathe with you crushing her!"

James? Who was...

Oh. Oh, *no*. It couldn't be *him*, could it?

Except his face was coming into sharper focus now, the blur resolving itself into features that were a masculine version of Harriet's. He had the same fine, classical nose, the same thickly-lashed blue eyes, and the same silky dark hair that had made his sister such a favorite with the gentlemen last season.

It was Lord Fairmont, and he was... dear God, he was lying on top of her!

"Lord Fairmont?"

"Yes?"

"Would you be so good as to get off of me?"

He blinked down at her. "I... yes. Yes, of course! I beg your pardon."

The weight atop her vanished, and she sucked in a quick, deep breath. Ah, yes, that was much better, except he'd had the gall to take his body heat with him. It was a great deal colder without him plastered against her, with the chill of the ground beneath her seeping into her back, and the brisk wind whipping goosebumps to the surface of her skin.

One might say what one liked about Lord Fairmont— he was arrogant, presumptuous, and far too enamored of his own opinions —but there was no denying he was exceptionally *warm*.

How did he contrive to be so warm? Was it because he was so tall? No, that didn't make sense. Perhaps it was that he was a well-built, muscular sort of man. Yes, that seemed likely. Harriett had mentioned once that he rode a great deal. Perhaps that was how he'd become so muscular, and...

Oh, dear. Her mind seemed to be wandering a bit.

"Can you sit up, Euphemia? Help her, James."

A warm, strong hand slid under her back, and the next she knew she was sitting upright. Her head felt far heavier than it should, and the world was tilting, but Lady Fosberry was there, and Harriett, and... yes, it was Lord Fairmont, just as she'd thought, although why he'd been on top of her remained a mystery.

Hopefully, no one had seen it, or there'd be no end to the gossip.

"Come, dearest, let's see if we might get you on your feet." Lady Fosberry reached for her hand. "You'll catch your death, sitting on the cold ground."

"Slowly, Miss Templeton." Lord Fairmont steadied his hand against her back. "You've had a nasty fall."

"A fall? What... oh, my goodness! There was a gentleman, in a yellow coat."

It was all coming back to her now. She and Lady Fosberry had come to Hyde Park to take a turn around the Ring, and a gentleman in a yellow coat had hailed Lady Fosberry. He'd been waving his hat in the air to get her ladyship's attention and had lost control of his pair.

The horses had broken loose, and they'd been

coming straight for her! The last thing she remembered she'd squeezed her eyes closed, and braced herself for a carriage accident.

Only it had never happened.

Lord Fairmont had appeared out of nowhere, and dragged her from the carriage! That was why he'd been lying on top of her! He'd wrenched her over the fence, and must have fallen on top of her when they hit the ground.

The ground, in the Ring. The Ring, which had been so crowded with carriages one could hardly stir an inch, and each of those carriages stuffed to bursting with members of the upper ten thousand, all of them on the hunt for the season's newest scandal...

Dear God. This mishap must have caused the most dreadful scene, and she'd been right in the middle of it! Already there was a buzz of excited voices around her.

Oh, she was afraid to look.

But there was no avoiding it, whether she chose to look or not, because as Lord Fairmont assisted her through the gate and back into the Ring toward Lady Fosberry's carriage— miraculously, it was still in one piece, and the frightened pair of high steppers now nowhere to be seen —she could feel the bodies pressing closer, and sense the weight of their gazes on her, and the barely-leashed excitement swirling like a thick fog around her.

This was a nightmare. They'd all seen her frozen with terror. They'd all witnessed Lord Fairmont's heroic rescue— had watched him clasp her in his arms, and...

They'd seen him *fall on top of her*.

She hadn't imagined she might remain inconspicuous this season— her family was too notorious for that —but whatever last shred of hope she'd had that the *ton* might permit her the barest modicum of privacy had now vanished.

They'd be gossiping about this for weeks to come, and her name was certain to figure prominently in the rumors, despite the entire debacle having been the fault of the gentleman in the canary yellow coat.

"Fetch Euphemia's shawl, Harriett, won't you? It's on the other side of the fence."

"Yes, of course!" Harriett scurried off, and Lady Fosberry cupped Phee's elbow in her hand and urged her toward the carriage door. "A hand for Miss Templeton, if you would, James."

"Of course." Lord Fairmont took Phee's hand, his fingers swallowing hers, and helped her into the carriage.

"Here you are, Phee!" Harriett hurried toward them with the shawl in her hand. Her brother assisted her into the carriage, and she sat down next to Phee, wrapping the shawl tenderly around her shoulders. "There. That's much better."

"Thank you." Phee clutched the shawl, pulling it more tightly against her neck. If only she could disappear beneath it! Lord Fairmont had paused to say a few words to Lord Gilbert, and the *ton* had taken the opportunity to gather near the carriage and gape at them. If she could have sunk between the blue velvet squabs, she would have done it in an instant.

At last Lord Fairmont swung himself up onto the box, and to her surprise, took the ribbons in hand.

"Is Lyman alright, James?" Lady Fosberry asked. "He's not hurt, is he?"

"No, he's fine. I asked him to take my phaeton and

pair to my lodgings in St. James's. After that debacle, I prefer to drive you all back to Fosberry House myself."

"Yes. I think that's best." Lady Fosberry gave an approving nod. "Shall we go, then? We must see Euphemia put to bed right away."

"There's no need." Phee squeezed Lady Fosberry's hand. "I'm perfectly fine, my lady."

And she was. The fall had knocked the breath clean out of her, yes, and her backside would be protesting for a few days, but she wasn't badly hurt.

Certainly not as badly as she would have been if Lord Fairmont hadn't appeared when he had. How remarkable, that he'd come just at the right time, and it had been quite heroic, the way he'd jumped into the fray without the least hesitation.

She glanced at him from the corner of her eye.

He hadn't spoken a word since he'd dismissed Lord Gilbert, but he was the sort of gentleman who didn't need to speak to communicate his displeasure. He sat upright in the box, his back rigid. His lips were pressed into a tight line, and his face was so cold and stony he might have been carved out of marble.

Not that he had much to smile about, given the state in which he'd found them this afternoon. He'd appeared equally as grim when they'd been introduced at the end of last season. He hadn't acquitted himself with much honor on that occasion, although to be fair, he'd just arrived home to find his sister in hysterics, the victim of a failed kidnapping attempt.

He'd had rather a lot to deal with this past year, hadn't he?

Perhaps she'd judged him too harshly. She knew herself that it was no easy task to act as the sole guardian of one's strong-willed younger siblings.

She didn't know much about Lord Fairmont, but Lady Fosberry had mentioned once that he'd only just turned eighteen when the full weight of an impoverished earldom and the care of his younger sister had fallen on his shoulders.

It couldn't have been easy for him. He was a trifle gruff, yes, but surely that was forgivable, given the burdens he—

"Lady Fosberry, wait!"

Phee turned at the shout. It was the gentleman in the yellow coat, waving them down.

"Good Lord, now what?" Lord Fairmont muttered, jerking the carriage to a stop. "Hasn't he caused enough trouble?"

The gentleman— Lord Gilbert —made an awkward dash toward them, stumbling over his own feet as he came. One of his cheeks was streaked with dirt, and the left sleeve of his bright yellow coat was torn.

"Lady Fosberry." He ran up to the side of the carriage, panting. "I'm so dreadfully sorry about the mishap. I was—"

"Mishap?" Lord Fairmont looked down his perfectly aristocratic nose at the man. "Is that what you'd call it, Gilbert? A bit short of the mark, I think."

"Yes, I—I mean no! Of course, it was a great deal worse than that, as you rightly point out, my lord." Lord Gilbert flushed up to the roots of his hair. "I beg your pardon for detaining you, but I couldn't let you leave without expressing my most sincere apologies."

"Are you quite alright, Lord Gilbert?" Lady Fosberry offered him a kind smile. "You weren't injured in the mishap, I trust?"

"Not a bit, no, which I daresay is more than I deserve."

"Indeed," Lord Fairmont muttered. "Far more."

Lady Fosberry cast a quelling glance at her nephew, then turned back to Lord Gilbert. "And your horses, my lord? Are they alright?"

"I think so, yes. They're, er, a trifle high-spirited, you see." Lord Gilbert flushed even redder, his gaze sliding to Phee. "The young lady isn't hurt, I hope?"

"She's fine, no thanks to you, Gilbert," Lord Fairmont snapped.

"*James!*" Harriett cried. "I do beg your pardon, Gilly. My brother is distraught."

"Not a bit, Lady Harriett. Lord Fairmont is quite right. Quite right, indeed." Lord Gilbert glanced at Lord Fairmont, his throat moving in a swallow. "May I have your permission, my lord, to call on you all later, so I might reassure myself of the ladies' health?"

"Of course, you—" Lady Fosberry began, but Lord Fairmont interrupted her.

"No, you may not. Now stand back, Gilbert." With that cutting reply, Lord Fairmont touched the ribbons to the horse's backs, and they were off, leaving poor Lord Gilbert stammering and stuttering behind them.

"For pity's sake, James!" Harriett exclaimed. "Was it necessary to speak so rudely to him? Anyone can see he's mortified. Poor Gilly."

Lord Fairmont jerked his head toward her, his jaw falling open. "Poor *Gilly*? For God's sake, Harriett, save your pity for those deserving of it. He might have killed someone today!"

"He didn't mean any harm, James! It was an accident." It took a great deal to rouse Harriet's temper, but she was fuming. "There was no reason for you to be so cruel to him!"

"I beg to differ. A gentleman who can't handle his team has no business in the Ring."

Harriett stared at him for a moment, then shook her head. "I'm ashamed of you, James."

If the afternoon hadn't already been ruined, that would have done it. Lord Fairmont flinched, but he said nothing in reply, and none of the rest of them ventured a single word after that.

They spent the drive from Hyde Park to Hampstead Heath in an oppressive silence.

Lord Fairmont was right, of course. It had been wrong of Lord Gilbert to venture into the Ring today — very wrong, indeed —yet despite his foolishness, Phee couldn't condemn him as harshly as Lord Fairmont.

She'd never seen a man more mortified than he, or more apologetic, his face flushed with misery as he'd stood before them, with his hat clutched in his hands. He'd made such a pathetic picture, that she couldn't find it in her heart to bear him a grudge.

"Phee? Are you coming?"

Harriett's voice startled her from her musings, and she looked up to see they'd arrived at Fosberry House. "Yes, of course."

She reached for her shawl, which had slipped from her shoulders and fallen to the floor of the carriage, then accepted the hand Lord Fairmont offered her, hiding her wince as her sore backside protested.

"Come, Euphemia." Lady Fosberry called, bustling toward the house. "It's straight to your bedchamber for you. James, if you'd be so good as to take her arm."

"Miss Templeton." Lord Fairmont offered his arm.

"Thank you, my lord. You acquitted yourself with admirable heroism this afternoon."

"There was nothing heroic about it, Miss Templeton," he replied curtly. "I did only what any proper gentleman would have done, under the circumstances."

She glanced up at him. His blue eyes were so like Harriett's, but he lacked his sister's warmth, and unless she was mistaken, he'd just made rather a point of saying he hadn't assisted her today for *her* sake. "Er, yes, of course."

Once they reached the door, he gave her a cold bow. "I wish you a quick recovery, Miss Templeton."

"Thank you, my lord."

"My dearest girl, you scared the life out of me today!" Lady Fosberry took her hand and hurried her upstairs to her bedchamber. "Are you quite sure you're alright?"

"Yes, just a trifle sore. I daresay it looked a good deal worse than it was."

"Yes, well, it looked perfectly appalling, I assure you. I nearly fell into a swoon. I'm afraid the *ton* won't soon forget it, either." Lady Fosberry let out a sigh as she sat down on the edge of the bed. "The season hasn't gotten off to a particularly promising start, has it?"

"I wouldn't despair quite yet, my lady. Today's mishap was regrettable, but it won't impact Harriett's prospects. She was merely an innocent bystander."

"That's, ah, not precisely true. You recall, Euphemia, that just before Lord Gilbert hailed us, I told you Harriett had developed a *tendre* for a gentleman other than Lord Farthingale?"

"Yes. You didn't get a chance to say who, but who-

ever it is, I can't imagine he could be any worse than...
oh. Oh, *no.* You don't mean—"

"I'm afraid so."

"Lord Gilbert?"

"Cecil Herbert, Viscount Gilbert. His acquaintances call him Gilly."

"But *how*?"

Lady Fosberry gave a helpless shrug. "All I can tell
you is that he and Harriett met at Lady Hampton's
house party this past summer, and soon enough they
were inseparable."

"My goodness. He's not at all the sort of gentleman I imagined Harriett could ever fall in love
with." It wasn't that there was anything wrong with
Lord Gilbert, but he had none of the smooth gallantry
of Lord Wyle, that had so dazzled Harriett.

He was a bit vulgar, and rather clumsy, as if he
hadn't yet worked out how to use his long limbs. His
clothing was garish and ill-fitting, and his manner
that of an overgrown boy— that is, much too eager to
be fashionable.

"Yes, I thought it odd at first, too," Lady Fosberry
said. "But despite Gilly's rather poor showing this
afternoon, he's a truly lovely gentleman."

He did have a rather sweet way about him. "Then
you approve the match?"

"I do, yes. Viscount Gilbert and Harriett have a
great deal in common. They both lost their parents at
a young age and were raised by overprotective
guardians— an elderly maiden aunt, in Gilly's case.
Miss Gratrakes is a worthy woman, but rather a
recluse, I'm afraid. Gilly was kept away from London
and fashionable society throughout his childhood."

"So that's why he's..."

"A bit of a bumbler? Yes. Well, that and he had the misfortune to fall in with a fast crowd at Oxford, who have encouraged his foibles for their own amusement. But you won't find a kinder gentleman than Lord Gilbert. He's rather a treasure."

Ah. Now she understood how it was.

For as long as Phee had known her, Lady Fosberry had been a collector of people the *ton* had discarded. Lord Gilbert was one of her misfits, it seemed, just as Phee and her sisters had been.

"Harriett and Lord Gilbert both have a charming air of naivete about them that's unusual in aristocratic families," Lady Fosberry went on. "They're uniquely suited in temperament, each of them being as kind, sweet-tempered, and apt to be pleased by everyone and everything as a pair of puppies."

"That certainly describes Harriett." She'd never known a lady with a sunnier disposition than Harriett's.

"But most importantly, Euphemia, Harriett is in love with him, and he with her. I believe both their happiness depends on this match. So, you see, we have a bit of a problem."

They did, indeed. "Lord Fairmont doesn't approve of the match?"

"Approve it? My dear girl, Lord Fairmont hasn't the vaguest idea about any of it. Even if he had been inclined to approve it, this afternoon's debacle would have changed his mind."

"He's rather stern, isn't he?" Too stern by half, but she kept that opinion to herself.

"More so than he used to be, yes. Poor James has been sadly out of sorts since he returned to England."

"With Harriett, you mean?"

40

"That's part of it, yes. Harriett was little more than a child when he left, you know. He doesn't know what to make of her now, and he fears losing her. But it isn't just that. James doesn't fit in amongst his old friends anymore, either."

"Why shouldn't he?" If anyone fit the mold of the fashionable, aristocratic gentleman, it was Lord Fairmont.

"Because, dearest, James is no longer an idle aristocrat. Unlike most gentlemen with ancient and honorable titles, he was obliged to work to replenish the family coffers. Some of his old friends look down on him for that, and those that don't, well..." Lady Fosberry gave a helpless shrug. "He has nothing in common with them anymore. He finds their frivolousness and self-indulgence contemptible."

Well then, she had something in common with Lord Fairmont, after all.

"So, you see how it is, Euphemia. Harriett and Lord Gilbert need your help."

"But what am I to do about it?" Lord Fairmont was hardly going to listen to *her*.

"Why, you must help me find a way to bring James around, of course. You're very clever about such things." Lady Fosberry patted her hand. "I feel certain you'll come up with some way to reconcile him to the match."

"Me? You want *me* to convince him?"

"Not convince him, precisely, but between the two of us, I daresay we can nudge him in the right direction."

Nudge Lord Fairmont? How?

Phee fell back against the pillows, her head muddled, and a dark foreboding gathering over her like a raincloud. There were dozens of different ways in which this could go wrong, and God knew anything that *could* go wrong, *would* go wrong.

Why, oh *why*, couldn't a single courtship ever go smoothly?

And how did she keep finding herself caught in the middle of them?

CHAPTER
FOUR

A self-imposed period of private reflection was usually enough to restore Phee's equilibrium and quiet the chaos in her mind.

It had always worked well enough at home. A brief period to herself when one of her younger sisters tried her patience was generally enough to cool her temper, but as it turned out, private reflection was, alas, no match for the tangled web that was the London season.

The instant she tugged on one of the snarled threads of this business between Harriett and Lord Gilbert, another one tightened. She'd been laying on her back atop her bed with her hands folded over her stomach since Lady Fosberry left her several hours ago, her thoughts chasing each other around inside her head like a dog with a bell tied around its tail.

She rose from the bed with a huff and paced restlessly to the window. It was another lovely day— it had been a remarkably sunny spring so far. The cherry blossoms, fooled by the warmer weather were already beginning to bud, but even the sight of the

43

cheerful pink flowers preparing to burst into bloom didn't brighten her spirits.

Despite what Lady Fosberry and Harriett believed, she *wasn't* clever. Not about people, at any rate, and certainly not when it came to matchmaking. She hadn't predicted a single successful match since Lady Fosberry had offered Juliet a season, and all this nonsense had started. The matchmaking had begun as a joke, for pity's sake! It was never meant to be a foolproof method of finding husbands.

Her sisters had all made spectacular matches, yes, but they'd secured them on their own, by being lovely, clever, and kind. She hadn't had a thing to do with it.

The only lady she'd ever attempted to match was Harriett, and she'd made a grand mess of it. What if she stuck her nose into this business with Harriett and Lord Gilbert, and the same thing happened again? She loved Harriett as if she were one of her own sisters. How could she bear to be the cause of ruining her happiness forever?

She already knew the answer.

She *couldn't*. If Harriett were to be hurt again because of some action she'd taken, she'd never forgive herself.

Lord Fairmont might be stern and arrogant, but he *was* Harriett's brother and her guardian. It was only right that he should manage his sister's affairs. No doubt he'd make a tangled mess of the thing before it was resolved to everyone's satisfaction, but Lady Fosberry would make certain Harriett wouldn't be made miserable by his choice.

Well, that was the thing settled, then.

She'd reached the end of this matchmaking business, for good this time. The only thing left to do now was inform Lady Fosberry of her decision.

She'd feel so much better once she had it over with. Yes, indeed, she'd just march downstairs right now, find Lady Fosberry, and tell her... tell her...

That she was abandoning Harriett to her fate.

God above, what a coward she was! This was a poor return, indeed, for all her ladyship had done for her family, but surely, Lady Fosberry would understand. She knew better than anyone how high-handed her nephew was, how overbearing, and dictatorial.

It was madness to imagine he'd listen to *her*, in any case.

She made her way downstairs, her heart a throbbing lump in her throat, but the house was quiet. Aside from Watkins, the entryway was deserted. "Is Lady Fosberry about, Watkins?"

"No, Miss Templeton. Her ladyship went out to pay a call on Lady Henry."

"Oh, I see." She deflated as if someone had stuck a pin into her. "Thank you, Watkins."

She gave the butler a brisk nod, then turned to go back upstairs.

But the thought of her silent bedchamber waiting for her made her turn down the hallway that led to the library, instead. It was her favorite room in the house, but with one thing and another, she hadn't yet had a chance to visit it. A novel would take her mind off her worries.

E.T.A. Hoffman's *The Devil's Elixirs* was meant to be scandalously naughty. Lady Fosberry was certain to have a copy of it.

She paused in the open doorway, inhaling the

soothing scent of leather and paper, but just as she was crossing the room to the tall bookshelves that housed the novels, the strike of a piano key caught her attention.

Someone was home, after all. Harriett, most likely.

There was another plink of keys, then a rapid series of scales as the player warmed up her fingers, and a moment later the strains of the opening aria from *The Barber of Seville* floated from the music room.

Yes, that was Harriett. She played like a dream.

Phee crossed the hallway, but just as she put her hand on the knob to enter the music room, a very fine voice launched into the "Largo al Factorum," the baritone swelling into the music room and spilling out into the hallway.

Now that was certainly *not* Harriett.

Goodness. Whoever he was, he had a remarkably fine voice.

The door had been left open a crack, and she peeked into the narrow gap in hopes of seeing the singer, but not wishing to interrupt.

Harriett was seated at the piano bench, and standing at her side was Viscount Gilbert, a smile on his face, and the loveliest voice imaginable emanating from his open mouth. It rolled through the room like a gentle wave, filling every corner with music.

She stared at him, amazed. None of the clumsy awkwardness from this afternoon was in evidence *now*, none of the stuttering or flustered bumbling. He was relaxed and confident, managing the brisk pace and complicated rhyme scheme of the piece with perfect, flawless confidence.

It was glorious. Not just his voice, which was one

of the finest she'd ever heard, but also the unfettered joy on his face as he sang, his gaze fixed on Harriett.

Fixed on her, as if... she leaned in, pressing her face into the narrow gap.

As if the only thing in the world that gave him more pleasure than the music was Harriett's face.

Harriett is in love with him, Euphemia, and he with her...

Lady Fosberry had told her Harriett and Lord Gilbert were in love, yes, but to hear a thing, and to witness it for oneself was *not* the same, particularly when it came to matters of the heart.

One had only to look at Lord Gilbert to see the love there— the light in his eyes, the softness in his features, the raw emotion in his voice that was reflected so plainly in his face. It was just the same expression with which her brothers-in-law looked at her sisters.

It was a look so beautiful, so tender, so utterly touching in its purity that a rush of tears filled her eyes. Lord Gilbert was madly, deeply in love with Harriett, and why shouldn't he be? Harriett was as sweet and kind a young lady as anyone could ever find.

As for Harriett's feelings for the viscount...

Harriett's back was to the door, but there was a looking glass just opposite the piano, and a glance revealed a tender smile, a sweet flush of pleasure on Harriett's cheeks.

That smile said more than words ever could. That was the besotted smile of the lovelorn.

She hadn't seen Harriett smile like that since that awful business with Lord Wyle.

If there was any doubt, Harriett's reaction as the

last magnificent note left Lord Gilbert's lips banished it forever.

"Oh, Gilly, that was *wonderful*!" She jumped to her feet, clapping her hands together. "I've never heard anyone sing it so well as you!" She gazed up at the viscount as if he'd just plucked a star from the sky, and placed it in her palm.

He took her hand and brought it to his lips. "You're too kind, Lady Harriett," he murmured, pressing a chaste kiss to her knuckles. "I've always enjoyed singing, but never so much as when I sing to you."

Phee suppressed a sigh. Goodness, they were utterly charming together, weren't they?

Who was she, to turn her back on something so beautiful, so powerful?

Why, no one. No one, at all.

Even more to the point, neither was Lord Fairmont.

But this wasn't the time to dwell on that. The last thing she wanted was to get caught spying on them. The singing had ceased, the room beyond the door falling silent, so she pulled the music room door closed as quietly as she could, then turned back toward the library, but she hadn't made it two steps before she smacked directly into a wall.

"Good afternoon, Miss Templeton."

"Oh!" She jumped back, patting her chest. "I beg your pardon."

Large, strong hands reached out to steady her, and she found herself looking up into a pair of dark blue eyes. Ah, not a wall, then, but an earl. An arrogant, tiresome earl, with an arrogant, tiresome smirk

48

on his too-handsome lips. "Lord Fairmont! You startled me."

"Eavesdropping, were you? I thought better of you than that, Miss Templeton."

Not much better, if the curl of his lip was any indication. "I thought better of *you*, my lord, than to be skulking about the hallways, sneaking up on people."

"Gentlemen don't *skulk*, Miss Templeton."

"Do you prefer creeping, my lord? Loitering? Prowling? Do feel free to choose a verb you approve of."

Lord Fairmont was not, it seemed, in the mood for linguistic fisticuffs, because he ignored this completely. "Have you seen Harriett? We're meant to have a walk together this afternoon."

"Er..." She cast an anxious glance behind her, but there wasn't so much as a single peep from the other side of the door now.

The music room had fallen suddenly, and suspiciously silent.

Either Harriett and Viscount Gilbert had heard Lord Fairmont's voice and wished to escape detection, or there was something else— something a trifle less innocent —unfolding on the other side of that door.

Thank goodness she'd managed to close it before Lord Fairmont came creeping down the hallway! She couldn't permit him to find Harriett and Lord Gilbert in there alone, or he'd have Harriett packed up and on her way back to Hereford before she could draw a breath.

"Miss Templeton? I asked if you'd seen Harriett."

She jerked her gaze back to him. "Harriett, my lord?"

"Yes, Miss Templeton. My *sister*, Harriett. You do remember her, do you not? A young lady with blue eyes, and dark hair?"

"No— ah, that is, of course, I remember her, my lord, but I haven't seen her. No indeed, I have not. She's not in the music room if that's where you were thinking of looking. I was just in there, you see, and it's utterly deserted." She caught his arm and began to tug him down the hallway. "Shall we check the library?"

"*We*, Miss Templeton?"

"Yes. I'd be most happy to help you search for her." She hurried down the hallway, dragging him along behind her, and stuck her head into the library. "Harriett? Are you here? No, it seems not, my lord. I was just about to go into the gardens for a walk. Would you care to join me?"

He glanced down at his coat sleeve as if her hand was some strange and objectionable insect that had landed there, and he couldn't decide whether to swat it away or crush it entirely. "Join *you*, for a walk?"

Dear God, was there ever a more infuriating man? "Yes, my lord. Now that I think of it, I did see, er... someone scurrying about the garden from my bedchamber window earlier."

"Scurrying, Miss Templeton?"

"Yes, indeed." She tugged him down the corridor toward the entryway. "Perhaps it was Harriet. Yes, I daresay she's already outside, waiting for you."

CHAPTER
FIVE

I f James didn't know Miss Templeton to be a quiet, meek little mouse, he might suspect she was up to something.

What that something might be, he couldn't begin to guess, but one thing was certain. She didn't care for him any more than he did her, and thus there wasn't a chance she'd request his company if she could avoid it.

So, why had she invited him to walk with her?

Her manner was suspicious, as well. She'd glanced over her shoulder at least half a dozen times since they'd left the hallway outside the music room. "Are you looking for someone, Miss Templeton?"

She startled, as if she'd forgotten he was there, the guilty flush he'd noticed earlier once against flooding her cheeks. "Me? No, indeed. Who would I be looking for, my lord?"

The woman was maddeningly difficult to decipher, but that blush told a thousand secrets those lips would never utter. "I wouldn't presume to question your honesty, Miss Templeton, but it did occur to me that you might know where Harriett is after all, and are looking for her."

"Ah, so you *do* presume to question my honesty, then. I already told you, my lord, I haven't seen Harriett this afternoon."

"It's not like her to fail to appear as promised." Although God knew she'd become adept at avoiding him since he'd revealed his wishes concerning Lord Farthingale. If Harriett didn't wish to be found, he wouldn't find her.

He never would have guessed his sister could be so slippery.

"She was quite upset after that scene in the Ring." Miss Templeton turned down one of the narrow, crushed stone paths that led from the main walk to the fountain in the center and sank onto one of the stone benches there. "Perhaps she merely needs some time to herself, my lord."

He seated himself beside her. "I daresay you agree with her that I was too harsh with Viscount Gilbert." Perhaps he had been, but damn it, a proper gentleman knew how to control his horses. It was a bloody miracle no one had been hurt.

"You might have been kinder about it, certainly, but in the moment, time was of the essence. Indeed, I thought you managed the whole thing rather neatly."

He glanced at her, surprised. "A compliment, Miss Templeton? Be careful, or I might begin to think you don't despise me, after all."

"I don't despise anyone, Lord Fairmont."

"I find that hard to believe." Everyone despised *someone*, and usually more than one someone, and he'd certainly never given her any reason to think kindly of him.

Which was just as it should be. He'd never sought Euphemia Templeton's friendship, and he didn't seek it now. He would just as soon his aunt had never involved the woman in their affairs.

"Then I'm sorry for you, my lord."

She was sorry for *him*? The infamous Euphemia Templeton, the lady all of London was gossiping about, who couldn't take a drive in Hyde Park or set foot inside a ballroom without everyone staring at her, and whispering behind her back, was sorry for *him*?

He took her in, assessing her from head to toe.

Gray. Everything about her was gray. Her bonnet, her pelisse, and the day dress she wore underneath it. A lady with such remarkably dark blue eyes should wear blue at every opportunity, but she dressed as if she wished to make herself invisible.

It was... well, it was none of his business, that's what. She might wear a flour sack if she liked. It was no concern of his. Still, given her aversion to attracting attention, it was astonishing that she'd even come to London at all.

He wouldn't have, if he'd been in her place.

"Tell me, Miss Templeton, what possessed you to come to London for the season? Why not remain in... Oxfordshire?"

Or wherever it was she'd come from.

"Kent, my lord."

"Yes, very well. Kent, then. My aunt gave me to understand that you don't care much for London."

"No, not much."

Well, then. That was as good an opening as he was likely to find. "It's fortunate we've find ourselves

53

here this afternoon, Miss Templeton. I wish to have a private word with you."

"A *private* word?"

"Yes, if you'd be so good."

"I can't think of a single thing you need to say to me that requires privacy, my lord."

"No? How unimaginative of you. I think we have quite a lot to discuss, after Harriett's catastrophic first season. You do remember her first season, do you not, Miss Templeton?"

She glanced down at her hands. "I'm not likely to soon forget it, my lord."

"I should hope not. But it's done now, and there's nothing to be gained by dwelling on that unpleasant business. My question for you, Miss Templeton, is this: Why have you come to London?"

She blinked. "I... forgive me, Lord Fairmont, but I don't understand."

"No? How curious. It's a simple question. What," he repeated, enunciating clearly, as he would do if he were speaking to an exceptionally dull child, "possessed you to come to London? Do you intend to marry this season?"

"*Marry*! Are you making fun of me, Lord Fairmont?"

Making fun? What did she mean, and why was she glowering at him as if she'd happily drown him in his aunt's fountain? "I have no idea what you're talking about, Miss Templeton."

"I imagine there are few things more amusing to a fashionable gentleman like yourself, Lord Fairmont, than a confirmed spinster coming to London in search of a spouse."

"How absurd. You can't be more than nineteen or twenty at the most. Hardly a spinster."

She was a meddlesome, interfering sort of lady, but he hadn't encountered many spinsters with as agreeable a face as hers, and that was to say nothing of the firm body he'd held against his when he'd rescued her in the Ring.

She'd fit nicely into his arms, her slender curves softening his sharp angles, so much so he'd—

Ahem. There was no sense in dwelling on that because it would never happen.

"I'm twenty-four, my lord, and I'm in London because your aunt and sister requested my presence here. I thought you knew that already."

"I'm aware of it, yes. What I fail to understand, Miss Templeton is why, after the utter mess you made of Harriett's first season, you didn't refuse the invitation. Under the circumstances, I'd think you'd have the decency to keep your distance. Indeed, I can't account for your presence here at all."

Her jaw dropped open. "You mean to say you're blaming *me* for that dreadful business with Lord Wyle?"

"Not entirely, no, but you were Harriett's matchmaker, were you not? That's what Harriett keeps telling me, at any rate. Surely, the matchmaker is at least somewhat responsible when the match goes awry?"

"You say the word "matchmaker" as if you're uttering a curse, my lord."

"Forgive me. I don't know much about your... how would you refer to it, Miss Templeton? The *art* of matchmaking? Or is it more of a business? My aunt certainly seems to be clamoring for your services. I daresay matchmaking can be quite lucrative."

She went still beside him. "Are you accusing me of *cheating* your aunt in some way, Lord Fairmont?"

Her face was turning an alarming shade of red. Perhaps he'd gone a step too far. "I'm not accusing you of a thing, aside from being bad at matchmaking, Miss Templeton."

"If you object so strenuously to my presence here, Lord Fairmont, you might have made your aunt aware of it before I came to London for the season."

"If I'd had the faintest idea you were coming, I would have. But it's too late now. You're here, and the damage is, unfortunately, already done. Still, I wish to make one thing clear to you, Miss Templeton."

She crossed her arms over her chest. "I'm listening, my lord."

"Under no circumstances will I permit you to meddle in my sister's marriage prospects. She doesn't need a *matchmaker* any longer, Miss Templeton. As her brother, I am the proper person to manage her affairs."

For an instant, she didn't react, but then, incredibly, she laughed.

Laughed, at *him*. "I fail to see what's so amusing, Miss Templeton."

"Why, your arrogance, my lord. If you imagine anyone other than Harriett will decide whom she marries, then I'm afraid you're in for a rather unpleasant surprise."

"Be that as it may, Harriett is no longer your concern."

He took care to use his coldest voice, the one that

56

made even the most arrogant of gentlemen blanch, but she didn't even seem to notice it. The timid little mouse had more of a backbone than he'd thought.

"Very well, my lord. Have you said all you wished to say?"

"Very well? That's it? No arguments? No protestations that Harriett can't possibly make an advantageous match without London's most celebrated matchmaker at her side?"

She raised an eyebrow. "You almost sound disappointed."

"Skeptical, perhaps." He didn't care for that stubborn little pinch at the corners of her lips, as if she knew something he didn't.

"Would you feel better if I argued with you, my lord? Stamped my feet and shook my fists?"

"I'd prefer you didn't. I abhor theatrics."

"Then I wish you luck this season, my lord." She smiled, her pink lips curling into something positively diabolical. With that, she rose from the bench, offered him a curtsey, and hurried off down the footpath, vanishing around the corner of the house and leaving him gaping after her, like a proper fool.

But surely, he'd made himself clear?

Yes, certainly he had. Miss Templeton couldn't possibly have misunderstood him.

Why, then, did he have the uneasy feeling that she'd just put him in his place?

～

"THEATRICS! HE ABHORS THEATRICS, HE SAYS." Phee stomped around the corner, sucking in a deep breath once she was out of Lord Fairmont's sight. "He'll have a merry time of it this season, then!"

That thought should have cheered her up, but her blood was boiling, and her fists were so tight that her fingers were going numb. She wasn't quick to anger, but it hadn't taken more than a dozen words for Lord Fairmont to set her temper alight.

"Bad at matchmaking, indeed!" She slumped against the side of the house, still panting with fury. "Meddle in Harriett's marriage prospects! *Meddle*, he says!"

Lord Fairmont was in for an unpleasant surprise, because if she hadn't *quite* made up her mind to help Harriett in her quest for true love, then she'd certainly made it up *now*.

What did he *mean*, accusing her of cheating Lady Fosberry, and warning her away from Harriett? Why, the man had as good as ordered her to leave London!

Yes, it was unfortunate what had happened last season— very unfortunate, indeed. No one denied that, but he'd laid the entire blame for it squarely on her shoulders.

Surely, that was unfair of him?

No one in London had the vaguest notion that Lord Wyle was hiding such enormous debts. If the worst of the gossips didn't know of his circumstance, then how was she expected to have known of it? Lord Wyle had been last season's Nonesuch, for goodness' sake! A paragon of virtue, a man of spotless reputation, and goodness knew he'd played the gallant gentleman to perfection. Why, he even looked the part!

How could she have known a devil lurked behind those angelic blue eyes? Did Lord Fairmont imagine she was some sort of mystic, who could see what others couldn't? Despite what the *ton* said, she was no sorceress.

If ever a man deserved a set down, it was Lord Fairmont. How humbling to find that the sweet, tender interlude she'd witnessed between Harriett and Gilly in the music room was less an inducement to meddle in Harriett's matrimonial affairs than her thirst to teach Lord Fairmont a lesson was.

Still, there was a *tiny* part of her, an insistent, niggling voice that kept whispering in her ear that perhaps there was just a *smidgen* of truth in what he said.

She'd been the one to suggest Lord Wyle as a match for Harriett. If she'd kept that opinion to herself, Harriett might never have developed a preference for the man. Young ladies were suggestible, and they'd hardly been in London a week before Harriett declared herself enamored of him.

Of course, so had every other young lady in London.

But that didn't change the fact that Phee had been the one who'd planted that seed in Harriett's mind, and she'd also encouraged the match. Didn't that make her in some sense responsible for the disaster that had followed?

Lord Fairmont might be an arrogant, condescending villain, but the truth was, she didn't have any business meddling in Harriett's affairs. That had been true last season, and it was even more so this time, now that Lord Fairmont was here.

What was she to do, then? How could she in good conscience abandon Harriett to the stormy seas of the marriage mart, when she knew Harriett was madly in love with Gilly? Her blasted conscience, the contrary thing that it was, wouldn't allow her to interfere this time, but neither would it permit her to turn her back on her dear friend.

Goodness, what a conundrum!

What was she to do? How was she to help Harriett?

She made her way past the eastern lawn and began to mount the steps that led from a small terrace back into the library, but before she could gain the top step, one of the glass doors swung open, and Harriett appeared on the threshold.

"Phee! Is James gone?" She scanned the lawn behind Phee, her brow pinched.

"I believe so, yes." Phee mounted the stairs, and followed Harriett into the library, closing the door behind her. "Hiding from him won't help matters, dearest."

Then again, if Harriett *was* hiding, Lord Fairmont was to blame for it, for treating his sister in such a high-handed manner. He didn't deserve her sympathy but try as she might, she couldn't erase the memory of his bewildered expression when he'd mentioned it wasn't like Harriett to break an engagement.

Cursed conscience. Nagging, useless thing.

"I know." Harriett threw herself into a chair with a dramatic sigh. "But he's so dreadfully interfering, Phee! I swear, if I have to hear Lord Farthingale's name one more time, I'll scream."

"He interferes because he cares about you, Harriett." She took a seat on the arm of the chair Harriett had plopped into, and rested a hand on her shoulder. "I wish I'd had someone who'd cared about me during my first season."

"I know, and I love him dearly for it, I just... I don't

like him much at the moment. He's an excellent brother— he always has been— but he's so stubborn! There are times when I'd dearly love to slap some sense into him."

Slap Lord Fairmont? Why, she couldn't imagine such a thing as...

Wait. Yes, she could. Indeed, it was tremendously satisfying, to imagine it.

"James's trouble is that he's so certain he's always right, that he dismisses any opinion that varies from his own. The maddening thing is, if he'd only give Gilly a chance, he'd see for himself what a sweet, wonderful man Gilly is. But after that scene in the Ring, I know he never will." Harriett looked up at her, her pretty blue eyes filling with tears. "What am I to do, Phee?"

"Oh, my dear. Don't cry. We'll find a way to make it right, I promise you."

"It isn't Gilly's fault he doesn't always know the proper way to act." Harriett dashed the back of her hand across her cheek. "If another gentleman would only give him a bit of advice, I'm sure he could be as charming as any other gentleman in London. More so, even."

"Yes, I think so, too." Lord Gilbert only wanted a bit of tutelage. She could help him polish some of his rough edges easily enough, but there were some things she couldn't do. The viscount's clothing, for instance, and his difficulties with driving, and a membership at White's.

He needed a gentleman for those things.

What a shame she'd sent Tilly and Kit off to Oxfordshire! Kit would have been a perfect choice to take Gilly in hand.

Ironically enough, so would Lord Fairmont.

He'd be ideally suited to such a task. Oh, he was rude, overbearing, and arrogant, to be sure, but there was no denying he was a gentleman of intelligence, taste, and fashion.

Harriett sniffled. "What's to be done, Phee?"

"I'm not sure yet, dearest, but your aunt and I will come up with something. If only it were a simple case of matchmaking, we could... oh, my goodness!"

She slapped her hand over her mouth. Why, of course!

It was the perfect solution! Why hadn't she thought of it sooner? Lord Fairmont had said it himself, when he'd insisted Harriett didn't need a matchmaker this season.

That was the truth. More true than Lord Fairmont could guess.

Harriett didn't need a matchmaker because she'd already found the gentleman she wished to marry. This season's task wasn't to find Harriett a proper match. Harriett and Gilly had already found each other, and made up their minds.

It wasn't either of *them* who posed a threat to the match. Neither of *them* was standing in the way of a happy ending.

Only Lord Fairmont was.

This season was about reconciling Lord Fairmont to the gentleman Harriett had set her heart on. It had nothing to do with matchmaking— at least, nothing to do with matchmaking Harriett and Gilly.

This season was all about matchmaking Gilly and *Lord Fairmont.*

Perhaps matchmaking wasn't quite the right word, but with a bit of finagling, and some judicious management, Gilly would gain the mentor he so desperately needed, and Lord Fairmont... well, at the very least he'd have someone to order about, but perhaps, in time and with a little luck, he'd find a friend in Lord Gilbert.

Lady Fosberry had said he didn't have many friends left. Really, it would be doing both of them a good turn—

"Phee? Have you got an idea?"

"I do, yes, but it's... well, to be honest, it's a bit daft."

"Those are always the best ideas. What are we going to do?"

Phee hesitated, her head spinning. Could she manage it? Perhaps the better question was, should she even attempt such a mad scheme? Lord Fairmont wasn't the sort of gentleman one trifled with. It could go spectacularly wrong, and if it did... well, this time she truly would have no one to blame but herself.

"Phee? Are you going to help me?"

One glance into Harriett's pleading eyes, and she had her answer. "We're going to do as we've always done, Harriett. We're going to matchmake."

Harriett's brow clouded. "Who? Me and Gilly? We're already matched."

"No. Not you and Lord Gilbert." Phee seized Harriett's hand. "Lord Gilbert and your brother. We're going to matchmake a friendship between Lord Gilbert and Lord Fairmont."

It wasn't going to be easy, however. Lord Fairmont already bore Gilly a grudge. He was certain to fight it every step of the way, but surely, he'd come around eventually.

He was an intelligent gentleman, after all.

Yes, he was certain to come around, sooner or later.

Sooner, with any luck. Whether they'd survive it until he did, however...

Well, that was another question entirely.

CHAPTER
SIX

For such an intelligent gentleman, Lord Fairmont was proving to be unforgivably dense.

Five days had passed since Phee's conversation with Harriett in the library. Harriett had called a truce with her brother directly afterward, setting aside her pique, and once again condescending to accompany him for their usual afternoon strolls in the garden.

Phee had watched them from her bedchamber window, wandering along the crushed stone pathways, engaged in what looked like a rather stilted conversation. Still, a stilted conversation was better than no conversation at all.

At least Harriett had been speaking to him again.

But alas, Lord Fairmont had wasted no time turning his small victory into a devastating defeat by doing something so awful— so utterly unthinkable —it was a wonder Harriett hadn't sunk her dinner fork into his hand tonight.

"Will you have more scalloped oysters, Lady Harriett?" Lord Farthingale took up the tongs, his hand hovering over the silver platter to his left.

Of all the offensive things Lord Fairmont might have done— of all the things that might have infuriated his sister —he'd chosen the most offensive one of all.

He'd invited Lord Farthingale to dinner this evening.

That sin alone was enough to warrant eternal damnation, but to make matters worse, Lord Gilbert, who was also in attendance had been obliged to give up his place beside Harriett and take the seat on Phee's left.

"No, thank you, my lord." Harriett glared across the table at her brother, her face as dark as a thundercloud. "I'm afraid I don't have much of an appetite this evening."

"Pity that," Lord Farthingale said with a shrug. "It is my considered opinion, Lady Fosberry, that not one cook out of a hundred can produce tolerable scalloped oysters, but these are acceptable. My compliments."

"That's, er, very kind of you to say, Lord Farthingale." Lady Fosberry gave him a pained smile.

No one seemed to have anything to say after that, and a tense silence fell over the table. Phee kept her gaze on her plate as she counted off the seconds.

One, two... a hundred, a thousand, a lifetime...

Dear God, had there ever been a more interminable dinner than this one?

She sneaked a peek at Lady Fosberry. Her ladyship had initially made a heroic attempt at pleasant conversation, but she'd since given it up as hopeless and subsided into a morose silence.

Harriett, who was seated to her aunt's right, had sat as still as a statue throughout dinner, only occasionally breaking her air of icy dignity to glare at her brother, who dared to look puzzled, as if he hadn't the vaguest idea what had put her out of temper.

The only one who seemed content was Lord Farthingale, who ate heartily, and without seeming to realize the only sound in the dining room was the scrape of his fork across his plate. "This glazed ham is a trifle sweet for my tastes, Lady Fosberry, but not ill-prepared."

Lady Fosberry took a half-hearted bite of the ham, then set her fork aside in favor of her wine glass. "I'll be sure to pass your effusive compliments on to my cook, my lord."

The ensuing silence that fell after this brief exchange lasted from the roasted fowl course through the lemon souffle. By the time Lady Fosberry rose to leave the gentlemen to their port, Phee had become so desperate to escape the table, that she was considering feigning a swoon.

"What does James *mean*, inflicting Lord Farthingale's presence on us without a word of warning?" Harriett demanded once they'd escaped to the drawing room. She was so enraged her voice was shaking.

"I confess I asked myself that same question." Lady Fosberry sank into a chair across from the settee. "James's friends are always welcome here, of course, but—"

"They're not friends, Aunt!" Harriett threw herself onto a settee with a huff. "James never once mentioned Lord Farthingale's name, until he decided I must marry the man! Dear God, how I feel for poor Gilly, trapped in the dining room, with James looking down his nose at him, and Lord Farthingale no doubt illuminating, point by point, all the ways in which the port falls short of his expectations."

"It's rather a grim picture, isn't it?" Lady Fosberry agreed with a sigh.

It must have been as grim as she predicted because the gentlemen appeared in the drawing room less than fifteen minutes later.

Poor Gilly looked a bit bemused, but his expression cleared as he caught Harriett's inviting smile, and he hurried across the room to her, casting Lord Fairmont a defiant look as he took a place beside her on the settee. "I've just got some new music, Lady Harriett. I hope you'll permit me to come and share—"

"You must tell me all you've been doing, Lady Harriett, since I last saw you in Hereford." Lord Farthingale swept across the drawing room in a cloud of cheroot smoke, and squeezed onto the settee on Harriett's other side, looking perfectly pleased with himself, his cheeks flushed from the port.

Harriett cast him a disdainful glance, and said only, "Nothing of any consequence, my lord."

"Nonsense, Harriett." Lord Fairmont managed a smile as he took a chair, but the edges of his lips were tight. "I'm sure Farthingale here would be delighted to hear all about your gardens, and the progress you've made on the pianoforte."

The chair he'd chosen happened to be a dreadfully uncomfortable one— Phee had made the mistake of sitting on it herself yesterday —and she couldn't smother a grin as she retreated to a distant corner of the drawing room, *The Devil's Elixirs* stuffed into a pocket of her gown.

A sore backside was no less than he deserved.

"The pianoforte," Lord Farthingale repeated, with ill-disguised impatience, but he quickly recovered himself, clearing his throat. "Er, yes, of course. I'd be delighted to know all about it, Lady Harriett."

"Indeed, I'm certain Harriett would love nothing more than to enlighten you, but first, Lord Farthingale, you must satisfy my curiosity about this new carriage you've commissioned. Do come and sit closer to the fire, and tell me all about it." Lady Fosberry patted the empty seat beside her. "Lord Fairmont tells me it will be the height of elegance, and I can't rest until I know every detail."

"It will be the most splendid equipage, my lady." Lord Farthingale jumped up from the settee, abandoning Harriett in an instant. "Far superior to any other in London."

Bless her, Lady Fosberry had just doomed herself to an evening of listening to Lord Farthingale drone on about his exquisite taste in carriage fittings for Harriett's sake!

Quite a sacrifice it was, too, but it wouldn't do much good as long as Lord Fairmont insisted upon hovering over Harriett and Gilly, like a hungry wolf about to pounce upon a pair of unsuspecting sheep.

Phee glanced down at *The Devil's Elixir*, then back up at Lord Fairmont.

She'd promised to help Harriett, but just how far was a lady required to go to assist a friend in her romantic endeavors? Because taking on Lord Fairmont was tantamount to hurling herself directly into the wolf's clutches.

An irritable, sharp-toothed, arrogant wolf, at that.

It was, of all things, the very last one she wanted to do, but Harriett glanced so longingly at Gilly, and

Gilly had the most charmingly shy smile when he looked at her, and...

Dash it. She let out a sigh, set her book aside, and rose to her feet.

Who was she to stand in the way of true love?

Poor E.T.A. Hoffman would be obliged to wait once again.

She approached the settee where Lord Fairmont sat alone, gazing at the fire, his brows pinched together in a frown.

If he hadn't brought all his troubles on himself, she might almost have felt sorry for him.

Almost.

She set her shoulders, drew in a deep breath, and pitched herself directly into the wolf's dark, gaping jaws.

"Would you care for a game of chess, Lord Fairmont?"

~

JAMES HAD BEEN SHIFTING from his right arse cheek to his left, cursing whoever had allowed such a disgracefully uncomfortable chair into the drawing room when Miss Templeton spoke, a look of grim determination on her face. "Chess?"

"Yes." She waved a hand toward an oval table in a corner of the drawing room. A handsome chess set sat atop it, ready for a game. "You have heard of chess, have you not, Lord Fairmont?"

"You wish to play chess with *me*, Miss Templeton?" She'd hardly spared him a glance throughout dinner, and when their gazes had chanced to meet, hers had been distinctly frosty.

Why would she seek out his company?

"You appear surprised, my lord. I don't know why you should be. I'm fond of chess, and Harriett tells me you're a clever player."

"Don't let that polite invitation fool you, James," Lady Fosberry warned. "She's only asking you because she's beaten Harriett and me so often, neither of us will play with her any longer."

"Yes, and you and Harriett both are dreadfully sore losers," Miss Templeton said with a smile. "I daresay Lord Fairmont knows how to lose like a gentleman."

First an invitation, and now a compliment? She must think him dim, indeed.

Anyone could see she was attempting to lure him to the other side of the room, so Harriett and Lord Gilbert might snatch a few moments of privacy while his aunt kept Farthingale entertained.

It should have annoyed him— that is, it *did* annoy him —but he was beginning to rethink this business with Farthingale. He'd promised Harriett he'd never attempt to coerce her into marrying a gentleman who didn't make her happy.

Farthingale didn't. Not now, and likely not ever.

It wasn't surprising. What sort of gentleman went on at such tedious length about the construction of the bloody dash rail of his carriage, for God's sake? His poor aunt's eyes were glazing over.

Even he could see the man was a bit of an arse. He could no longer remember why he'd ever thought Farthingale would make a proper match for Harriett.

He returned his attention to Miss Templeton, who was still awaiting his answer. "What makes you think I'm going to lose, Miss Templeton? I rarely do."

"Neither do I, my lord. I'd be pleased to find a worthy opponent."

She gave him a small smile. His gaze dropped to her lips, and an unexpected quiver of awareness tripped down his spine. She was wearing one of her plain, somber gowns— this one a dull brown, instead of her usual gray.

Euphemia Templeton might hide all she liked. She might do whatever she could to persuade everyone there wasn't a single interesting thing about her, but one only had to look at her smile to see the lie.

That smile gave her away. It seemed to hold a world of secrets.

He rose to his feet and motioned toward the chess table. "I suppose we'll soon find out which of us is the wilier player, won't we?"

Wait. Were they still talking about chess? Because there was a curious gleam in her blue eyes he'd never seen before, and taken together with that smile... oh, Miss Templeton wanted to beat him at chess as badly as he did her, and he was more curious than he should be to find out which of them would emerge the victor.

He was more curious about *her* than he ought to be. When had that happened?

"White, or black, my lord?" She paused beside the table, her long, delicate fingers hovering over the pieces.

"Since I'm quite sure you've cast me as the villain, Miss Templeton, I'll take black." He gestured to the left side of the table, where the ebony pieces sat in a neat row on the board, ready for their first attack.

"Villain?" She took her seat, glancing up at him,

eyebrows aloft. "I've no idea what you mean, my lord. This is merely a friendly game of chess."

"That remains to be seen." He seated himself across from her, waving a hand at the board. "I await your first move, Miss Templeton."

She didn't hesitate but slid her pawn to E4 with the confidence of a lady who'd practiced her opening gambit.

He followed, predictably, by moving his pawn to E5. They shifted their pawns about for a bit, both of them avoiding any risky or unexpected moves, neither of them speaking as they took each other's measure.

It was promising to be the dullest game of chess imaginable, until at last she said, "I'm afraid Harriett was made quite unhappy by Lord Farthingale's presence at dinner this evening, my lord." As she spoke, she moved her knight across the board, threatening his pawn.

"Are you trying to distract me from the game, Miss Templeton? It won't work."

"I don't need such paltry tricks as that, I assure you, Lord Fairmont."

"As for Harriett, we agreed your, er... matchmaking services weren't required this season." He slid his knight forward to contest the center of the board, then raised his head to meet her eyes. "Harriett's matrimonial prospects are not your concern."

"I beg your pardon, my lord. We didn't *agree* on anything. You stated your opinion on the matter, and I said nothing at all." Without pausing to consider her move, she picked up her knight and dropped it directly behind her pawn.

He lifted an eyebrow. "Sacrificing your knight for

a measly pawn, Miss Templeton? Rather reckless, don't you think?"

"I prefer to play an aggressive game, my lord." She waited, hands folded primly in her lap as he moved his pawn, and took her knight. "It's curious that you took my silence the other afternoon for agreement. I wonder if you often make that same mistake with Harriett."

"My position regarding Harriett's marriage prospects isn't an *opinion*, Miss Templeton. It is, quite simply, what I expect to happen."

"I see. It occurs to me, Lord Fairmont, that you're in a position to do Lord Gilbert a good turn."

"Why in the world would I want to do that? I hardly know the man." He'd just as soon keep it that way, too. He didn't have any use for fools like Gilbert.

"Because he's a friend of Harriett's, Lord Fairmont, and because he'd benefit from the tutelage of a more experienced gentleman. One such as yourself."

"I'm not a nursemaid, Miss Templeton. Now, attend the game, if you please. You've just lost your knight."

"Have I? Dear me." She didn't hesitate, but moved her queen into position three spaces to the right of his pawn, as if she'd envisioned the move three turns ago. "Check."

"Wait." What the devil had just happened? He stared at the board and saw his mistake at once. When he'd moved to take her knight, he'd exposed his king and left his rooks, bishops, and queen no way out. How had he not seen it?

"Your mistake was in not risking your queen earlier, my lord. Right here." She tapped the empty square at E7. "If you'd done that, you'd have skewered my knight and pawn, and been in a position to threaten my king."

Patronizing bit of baggage. "Yes, thank you, Miss Templeton. I see it now."

"Alas, it's rather too late, I'm afraid. Chess isn't a game for the faint of heart, my lord. It's rather like the marriage mart that way. Don't you think so?"

"I do not. The marriage mart isn't a game, Miss Templeton, though I shouldn't be surprised that you find it so, playing at matchmaking as you do."

Oh, she didn't like that at all. She showed little outward reaction, but he could see her anger in the infinitesimal narrowing of her dark blue eyes as clearly as if she'd let out a shriek of rage, and upended the chess board onto the carpet, scattering the pieces everywhere.

He'd quite like to see that, now he thought of it, but first...

He seized his king, sliding it to E7, and taking it out of check. "Indeed, I'm surprised you've decided to remain in London, Miss Templeton. I hope it isn't because you intend to interfere with Harriett's season, despite my wishes. Unless I didn't make myself clear?"

"You made yourself perfectly clear, Lord Fairmont." She met his gaze directly now, that mysterious little smile flirting with the corners of her lips. "I promise you, I have no intention of attempting to matchmake Harriett this season."

"Well, then? Why do you stay? My aunt tells me the rest of your family is in Oxfordshire at the moment. I would think you'd wish to be with them."

"I already told you why, Lord Fairmont. I made a promise to your sister and your aunt that I would remain in London for the season. I won't go back on my word."

"Your services are no longer required, Miss Templeton."

"Not by you, perhaps."

What the devil did that mean? "I beg your pardon?"

"It may be true that my matchmaking services are no longer required, but my friendship is still very much necessary to Harriett. I wouldn't dream of abandoning her."

"I don't see why it should make any dif—"

"Forgive me, Lord Fairmont. You're Harriett's elder brother and guardian, but you're not *mine*, or indeed, anything else to me. You don't get to dictate where I may go, or where I may stay." Her blue eyes flashed. "I am your aunt's guest, and here I shall remain until either Harriett or Lady Fosberry expresses a wish otherwise."

He leaned back in his chair, taking in her pink cheeks, the way that flash of temper turned her eyes a darker blue. Well, it seemed the quiet, reserved Miss Templeton was hiding a bit of fire underneath that calm exterior.

She was good at that. At hiding.

Not just her temper, either, but everything that could distinguish her as anything other than the spinster she pretended to be. Her wit, the sharp edge of her tongue, those pretty blue eyes, and those distracting curves.

All at once, all those somber dresses began to make sense.

Miss Templeton was hiding in plain sight.

But *why*? What did she have to gain from—

"Bishop to E4, my lord."

He jerked his attention back to the board, and shifted his pawn, sacrificing it to keep his king safe. Not that it would do him much good. The game was effectively over.

She plucked his pawn from the board. "Do you not think, Lord Fairmont, that Harriett has a right to marry the gentleman she loves?"

He slid his king to F7, the only move available to him. "Harriett has led a sheltered life, Miss Templeton. She's too innocent to know what love is."

"You underestimate her, my lord." She slid her bishop forward to C4. "She knows her mind."

Perhaps she did, at that. Harriett had told him from the start that she didn't care for Farthingale, and since then, she'd never wavered. She was no longer the child she'd been when he'd left England, no longer the little girl he'd read stories to, and whose hurts he'd tended.

He'd missed so much of her life, and now, she no longer needed him. A pang sliced through him as he glanced over his shoulder at her. She was bent over a sheaf of sheet music, Lord Gilbert's fair head next to her dark, sleek one.

They almost looked as if they were—

"It's your move, Lord Fairmont."

He tore his gaze from Harriett and parried by moving his pawn to D5, but it only delayed the inevitable.

After that, it was over quickly in a flurry of bishops, pawns, rooks, and kings, until at last, Miss Templeton seized his queen. "Well done, Miss Templeton."

She didn't gloat—he'd give her that—but merely

toyed with his queen, rolling it between her fingers, the black ebony like a dark inkblot against her pale skin, until at last she set it aside and rose from her chair.

He looked up, holding her gaze with his. "Another game, Miss Templeton? It's only fair that you give me a chance to recover my wounded pride."

She smiled. "Perhaps another time, Lord Fairmont."

CHAPTER
SEVEN

S urely, a monk should know better than to sip a mysterious elixir from an ancient flask?

One would think so, but Medardus, in a moment of what Phee could only call acute madness, had just swallowed a worrying amount of the devil's elixir!

Well, no good would come of *that*, would it?

She flipped to the next page, and... ah ha! It was just as she'd thought. That one tiny sip had resulted in hallucinations, insanity, lust, murder, and all manner of wickedness. In the space of a single page, poor Medardus had quite lost his mind! What would become of the beautiful Aurelie now? How would Medardus evade his murderous twin, or defeat the sinister curse afflicting his family, or—

"Phee? Phee, are you here?"

Dash it. She'd just gotten to the best part!

"Phee, where are you?"

She sank lower in her chair as light footsteps hurried down the hallway. If someone should come in, they wouldn't be able to see the top of her head from the doorway, and they might go about their business and leave her alone with Medardus.

An instant later the library door flew open, and Harriett's cheerful voice shattered the quiet. "Oh, there you are, Phee. You must come at once!"

"Must I?" She smothered a sigh, and slipped a bit of paper between the pages of *The Devil's Elixir* to mark her place. At this rate, poor Medardus was destined to languish in a psychosis forever. "What's happened now? Have the goats gotten into Lady Fosberry's rose gardens again?"

"No, no. My aunt has arranged a surprise for me, and it's ever so much fun!" Harriett darted across the room, and seized her hand. "Come and see for yourself."

"Yes, alright." Phee cast one final, longing glance at her book, but she let Harriett tug her from her chair and hurry her down the hallway, through the dining room, and out the terrace door to the south lawn.

There, she came to an abrupt stop.

"My goodness, where did all these people come from?" There were at least two dozen of them meandering about, bright spots of color against the rolling ribbon of velvety green.

"My aunt said it was a shame not to take advantage of the lovely warm weather, so she put together a game of lawn bowls! It's just a few of our neighbors and some other friends. Isn't it delightful? My aunt is making up the teams. You'll play with me, won't you, Phee?"

She glanced over the knots of people scattered across Lady Fosberry's lawn. There'd been a time when she'd been rather good at lawn bowls, but that had been ages ago, and even then, she'd only ever played with family.

There were one or two familiar faces in the crowd gathered on the lawn, but most of the guests were strangers to her, and all of them terribly fashionable. The idea of all those prying eyes on her made a shudder roll down her back. "Perhaps later, dearest. I believe I'll just observe for now."

"Oh. Alright, then." Harriett's excitement dimmed for an instant, but then she glanced over Phee's shoulder, and brightened again at once. "You'll play, won't you, James?"

Phee jerked around, and there was Lord Fairmont, lounging against the stone wall beside a refreshments table that had been set up on the terrace. "Of course I'll play, Hattie, if you wish it."

"Wonderful! Aunt," Harriett called, as she skipped down the stairs. "James and I will make up a team!"

He didn't follow after Harriett, but strolled lazily toward her, his blue eyes inscrutable as they took in her plain, gray day dress with a thoroughness that made her squirm.

"Good morning, Miss Templeton."

What in the world was he staring at? It was most uncomfortable, that stare, as if he could see directly through her. "Lord Fairmont."

"What a pity you won't join the game, Miss Templeton. Do you not care for bowls? Or is it the company that offends you?"

Who was offended, for pity's sake? Not her. "I have no objection to either bowls, or to the company, but it's been ages since I played, and I would be sure to disappoint my partner."

"I see. And what will you do, while the rest of the party is playing at bowls?"

My, he was curious today, wasn't he? "I suppose I'll sit and chat with Lady Fosberry."

She waved a hand toward one end of the lawn, where a half dozen chairs had been arranged. Lady Fosberry sat atop one of them, a pencil in one hand and a bit of paper in the other, laughing with her guests as she sorted out the teams.

He raised an eyebrow. "You mean to say you prefer to sit all afternoon with a rug over your knees, and a cushion at your back? You're hardly an elderly maiden aunt, Miss Templeton. There's no need for you to act like one."

He didn't give her a chance to reply, but marched down the terrace steps, leaving her staring after him with her mouth agape. Maiden aunt! Who said she acted like a maiden aunt? God above, he was the rudest man imaginable!

Perhaps he wouldn't make a proper mentor for Lord Gilbert, after all. The last thing London needed was another unbearably arrogant gentleman.

She grumbled to herself as she made her way slowly down the stairs, taking care not to glance toward the knot of laughing young people who were making a great commotion over choosing their teams and selecting their bowls.

"My, that is a fierce frown, Euphemia." Lady Fosberry shaded her eyes from the sun as Phee approached. "Why so sour, my dear? And on such a pleasant day, too."

"I'm not at all sour, I assure you." Phee plopped down into the chair beside her ladyship, and under the guise of adjusting her skirts, took a moment to smooth her expression into its usual attitude of calm complacency.

It took more effort than it should have done.

If Lady Fosberry noticed, she didn't mention it, saying only, "You don't wish to play?"

For pity's sake, why was everyone so insistent she play at bowls? "No. They've already got five teams of two players each. I'll only upset the numbers if I play."

She'd be the odd one out, the spare. It was a position that had become increasingly familiar to her after her sisters had all married. She seemed to be forever on the outside, observing life unfold at a distance.

Not that she minded it, of course. She was fine as she was, observing from the sidelines.

Really, she preferred it here.

"If you wish to play, Euphemia, I'll partner you. I daresay we'd beat them all handily." Lady Fosberry tapped her lip, considering it. "Perhaps I should offer a prize for the winners."

"No, thank you, my lady. I'm perfectly content as I am." She did enjoy playing bowls, but she didn't fancy an afternoon trapped under Lord Fairmont's keen eye.

"Very well, then. If you're not going to play, shall we have some refreshments? I do adore those almond biscuits cook has—"

"Lady Harriett! Oh, Lady Harriett!"

The booming voice echoed across the lawn, cutting through all the chatter, and for a moment an abrupt silence fell over the party as every head turned at once toward the terrace.

There, at the top of the stairs stood Lord Gilbert,

wearing a bright, sky blue coat over a pink satin waistcoat, a fall of extravagant ruffles at his wrists and throat.

"Oh, dear," Lady Fosberry murmured, leaning close to Phee. "Whatever is he wearing?"

"I believe it's a coat. It's, ah, very bright, is it not?"

"Lady Fosberry! Thank you ever so much for the invitation, my lady!" Gilly approached and shook Lady Fosberry's hand with enough vigor to tear her arm from its socket. "You look exceedingly well, my lady. What a great relief it is to me, to find you've suffered no ill effects from our mishap the other day."

If Lady Fosberry thought his lordship's greeting a bit too enthusiastic to be proper, one couldn't tell it from the gracious smile she bestowed upon him. "I'm very well, indeed, Lord Gilbert."

"Wonderful, my lady, wonderful!" A beaming smile bloomed on the viscount's flushed face. "You can't imagine how pleased I am to hear it. Miss Templeton! How lovely to see you today!"

"How do you do, Lord Gilbert?"

"Very well, indeed. It's a pretty day, is it not?"

"Very pretty, yes." She blinked, dazzled by the bright blue glare assaulting her eyes.

Goodness, that coat was... well, she couldn't quite articulate it, but it had quite scrambled her brain.

Dear God. If there was ever a gentleman in need of fashion advice, it was poor Lord Gilbert. He was... how did one put it if they didn't wish to be unkind?

He was... eccentric? Yes, that was a proper word for him. Viscount Gilbert was *eccentric*. Some might even call him peculiar.

But what did it matter?

Despite his manners, it was difficult to fault so

agreeable a gentleman, or one so eager to make a favorable impression. He had none of the arrogance or thin-lipped condescension of so many of the *ton*.

Her gaze wandered over to Lord Fairmont.

Particularly the aristocratic gentlemen.

Lord Gilbert was a bit awkward, yes, and he'd much better do away with the lurid coats, but goodness knew a man couldn't always be accurately measured by his manner and clothing. Lord Wyle had been the epitome of the fashionable gentleman, and he'd turned out to be an utter scoundrel.

All that mattered was that Harriett was in love with Gilly, and he was equally besotted with her.

And what was love, if not an utter absurdity?

"Harriett is just over there, my lord." Lady Fosberry nodded toward the other side of the lawn, where Harriett was speaking to a group of young ladies. "Do go and greet her, won't you? She particularly asked that you be invited today."

"Did she, then?" He didn't wait for an answer, but tore across the lawn, the sun turning the bold blue of his coat nearly pearlescent. Goodness, that color quite seared one's retinas, didn't it?

She was no arbiter of fashion, but even she could see his dress was... not quite the thing.

Harriett didn't seem to notice anything amiss in his appearance, however. Her face lit up like the sunrise at the sight of him, and she waved him over with all the eagerness of a lady who was madly in love. "Lord Gilbert! How do you do? Come, you must join us for a game of bowls."

But if Harriett's smile was the sunrise, Lord Fairmont's frown was the thick, dark cloud that eclipsed it. He was too much the gentleman to scoff openly at

Lord Gilbert, but neither could he quite hide his irritation as Gilly tripped clumsily across the lawn, nearly falling on his face in the process, and approached them. "A perfect day for bowls, eh? I'd love to—"

"I'm afraid we've already made up the teams," Lord Fairmont interrupted. "Too bad, Gilbert. Perhaps the next game."

"Oh, of course. I beg your pardon. I don't want to upset your teams." Gilly glanced around, his cheeks flushing as he suddenly became aware that every eye was upon him, and noticed the smirks on the lips of several of the gentlemen. "I'll just, er..."

"Euphemia? My dear child, have you gone deaf?"

"Hmmm?" Phee jerked her gaze away from Lord Gilbert to Lady Fosberry, who'd evidently said her name several times, judging from the impatient expression on her face. "I beg your pardon, my lady?"

"Goodness, you were a thousand miles away, child. I asked if you wanted some tea."

"No, I..." She never finished the sentence, because the next thing she knew, she was on her feet.

She didn't plan it. She wasn't even aware she'd risen until she was halfway across the lawn. All she knew was that she recognized the embarrassment on Gilly's face, the flush of humiliation, because she'd felt it herself, too many times to count.

"If you wish to play, Lord Gilbert, I'll be your partner."

No one was more startled than she was when those words fell from her lips, but it was worth it when Gilly turned to her, and his embarrassment melted into a relieved smile. "Oh, Miss Templeton. Are you sure you wish to play?"

"Perfectly sure, yes."

"How good of you, Phee!" Harriett grasped her hand and gave it a thankful squeeze. "I couldn't have enjoyed the game if poor Gilly were excluded."

"Indeed, it's ever so kind of you, Miss Templeton!" Gilly bumbled a bit as he tried to shake her hand, seemingly without having the dimmest notion that shaking a lady's hand wasn't at all the thing.

"Not at all, Lord Gilbert. I'm quite mad for bowls."

"Oh, you must call me Gilly, Miss Templeton. I insist upon it." He beamed at her. "All my friends do."

"Very well." She smiled at him. "Gilly, then."

Lord Fairmont said nothing, but she could feel his hot gaze boring into the side of her face as she joined the party and accepted a bowl from Harriett.

She cast a withering glance at him, before turning to smile at Gilly. "I can't think of anything more pleasing than an afternoon of bowls."

"I DO BEG your pardon for being so hopeless at bowls, Miss Templeton." Gilly offered her an uncertain smile. "Perhaps I should have confessed it when you so kindly agreed to partner me."

Lord Gilbert was not— perhaps unsurprisingly — proficient at bowls. Still, what he lacked in skill, he more than made up in enthusiasm, and she couldn't find fault with him. "Indeed, Lord Gilbert, you needn't apologize. I can't recall ever enjoying a game of bowls more."

He grinned down at her. "Really? You don't mind losing?"

"Not a bit." They'd come in dead last, but she'd

accepted their dismal ranking cheerfully. The point of any game was to enjoy oneself, after all, and this afternoon she'd laughed until her sides ached.

Between the two of them, she and Gilly made quite a pair. She went about the business of bowls mathematically, taking the time to calculate the pitch of the lawn and the bias of her particular bowl before she tossed it, while Gilly hurled his about willy-nilly, flinging them with such abandon, that the other guests took to ducking and covering their heads when it was his turn, and Phee was in constant terror for the costly glass doors that led from the library onto the terrace.

"May I fetch you a glass of lemonade, Miss Templeton?" Gilly nodded toward the refreshments table. A knot of young people had gathered around it, talking and laughing as they sipped at lemonade and nibbled on cook's sweet almond biscuits.

Harriett was among them, her cheeks flushed a becoming pink from the exercise, and Lord Gilbert couldn't take his eyes off her.

"Come, let's go together, and I'll fetch one for Lady Fosberry, as well."

"Yes, let's." Lord Gilbert held out his arm, Phee took it, and they made their way to the refreshments table. Gilly helped her to two glasses of lemonade, then escorted her to the chair next to Lady Fosberry's before rushing off to join Harriett.

"My dear Euphemia, how kind you were to offer to partner Lord Gilbert." Lady Fosberry gave her an approving nod. "It was a great pleasure for me to see you join in the game today. It looked as if you enjoyed yourself."

"I did, very much. Lord Gilbert is every bit the delight Harriett says he is."

"He's lovely, isn't he?" Lady Fosberry watched as Gilly approached Harriett, a smile playing about the corners of her lips. "He's at his best when he forgets himself, and behaves naturally, as he did today."

"Yes. He's clever and funny— even charming, in his unique way." He was unfailingly kind, as well, even to those who weren't especially kind to him.

Lord Fairmont, for one.

Not that he was *unkind*, precisely. No, she couldn't accuse him of that. He wasn't rude to Gilly, or insulting in any way. For all Lord Fairmont's arrogance, he was too much a gentleman for such low behavior.

But neither did he single Gilly out for any particular courtesy. For the most part, Lord Fairmont ignored him, but more than once she'd caught him scrutinizing the viscount with an intensity utterly out of place for two gentlemen of such slight acquaintance.

If Gilly had noticed it, he hadn't remarked on it, nor had it seemed to affect his enjoyment of the game, but it had put her so out of temper, that it was all she could do not to toss her bowl directly at Lord Fairmont's head.

It was disconcerting, this sudden urge toward violence. She'd never wanted to maim an earl before, but this was the second time in as many days that Lord Fairmont had roused her temper.

She *did* have one, despite her calm appearance. Any one of her sisters could attest to that. They compared her to a hibernating bear, claiming she was quiet and peaceable until someone made the mistake of poking her.

Lord Fairmont seemed able to call her temper forth with nothing more than a smirk, despite the pains she took to hide it. Somehow, he'd managed to slip under her skin, and there he remained, poking away like a devil with a tiny pitchfork.

"You excel at bowls, Miss Templeton." As if she'd summoned him with her dark thoughts, Lord Fairmont dropped into the chair beside her. "If you'd had a different partner, you might have won."

Naturally, *he'd* come in first place. "I don't care about winning, my lord. I enjoyed myself. Surely, that's the point of any game?"

"It's a miracle you escaped an injury. I imagine bowls is far less enjoyable with a broken foot, or a crushed finger."

"Perhaps so," she gritted out. "But as you can see, my lord, my feet, and my fingers are very much intact."

He snorted. "Not from lack of trying on Lord Gilbert's part."

"Are you accusing Lord Gilbert of intentionally trying to injure me?" By God, she was holding on to her temper by a single, fraying thread.

He raised an eyebrow at her waspish tone. "I'm accusing him of carelessness, Miss Templeton. One would think he'd have learned his lesson after that debacle in the Ring."

"That was an *accident*, my lord."

"An accident that arose from carelessness, or rather recklessness, I should say. Lord Gilbert would do well to learn to behave like a proper gentle—"

He broke off as she leaped to her feet.

"A proper gentleman, Lord Fairmont? Is that what you were going to say?"

"Er, well—"

"Because I can't help but agree with you. Lord Gilbert could benefit greatly from the friendship of a gentleman who understands the intricacies of the fashionable world. A gentleman like *you*. It's a great pity that you prefer to sit here and criticize him, instead of offering your assistance to a gentleman who's such a dear friend of your sister!"

He gaped up at her, his eyes wide. "Did you just stamp your foot, Miss Templeton?"

Had she? Goodness only knew. "If I did, it's because you *deserve* it!"

Oh, dear. Her chest was heaving, her breath coming in great, panting gulps and the words were piling up behind her tongue, words she'd almost certainly regret.

She mustn't become overwrought. Dreadful things happened when she became overwrought, and already heads were turning in their direction.

She turned on her heel, preparing to march off and enjoy her temper tantrum in private, but her tongue had got the best of her now, and before she could hurry away, it delivered a final parting shot.

"Lord Gilbert's manners may leave something to be desired, Lord Fairmont, but so do yours, and it's a far worse failing in you because you *know* better!"

Had Euphemia Templeton just *scolded* him?

It had *sounded* like a scold, and given that she was marching off in what could only be described as high dudgeon, her skirts flying out behind her in outraged fury, he really could only come to one conclusion.

He turned to his aunt. "Euphemia Templeton just *scolded* me."

It had been a furious scold at that, as if he were a naughty schoolboy instead of the Earl of bloody Fairmont. No one had ever dared such a thing before, but Miss Templeton had stopped just shy of slapping his face with her glove, and challenging him to a duel!

"Honestly, James, it's no less than you deserve," his aunt snapped. "I swear, you could try the patience of a saint."

"Me? What do you mean? What did I do?" He was perfectly innocent, by God. "I merely complimented her on her proficiency at bowls, and the next thing I knew she'd jumped to her feet, and was shouting at me."

"Is that so? Because I would have sworn I heard

you mention Lord Gilbert's name. Something about recklessness, I believe, and broken fingers. Does that sound at all familiar, James?"

Was that what all the fuss was about? "Very well, then yes. I said he was reckless, and so he is! I'll be damned if I'll apologize for—"

"Don't make it worse by cursing, if you please. Your remarks about poor Lord Gilbert were uncalled for, James—"

"Poor Lord Gilbert!" For God's sake.

"They were uncalled for," she repeated as if he hadn't spoken. "Euphemia was right to scold you for it." His aunt pointed a shaking finger at the retreating form of Miss Templeton. "Do you realize, James, how difficult it is to make Euphemia Templeton lose her temper?"

"No." How should he? "I hadn't the vaguest idea such a quiet little mouse as Miss Templeton was hiding such a sharp tongue. You never mentioned *that*."

His aunt snorted. "Euphemia Templeton is no mouse, James. If you imagine she is, then you've quite mistaken the matter. I thought you were more perceptive than that."

"How could I have known? She hasn't said more than two dozen words in my presence since we arrived in London."

Then again, she'd had plenty to say to him last night, right before she'd trounced him at chess, hadn't she? And he'd caught a glimpse of a temper simmering beneath her placid expression when he'd accused her of playing at matchmaking, as well. There'd been a flash of it in her eyes, like the blue light at the base of a candle's flame.

What else was Miss Templeton hiding, behind those mild blue eyes and soft pink lips?

"It takes a great deal to rouse Euphemia's temper. Allow me to offer you my congratulations, James, for having the dubious honor of being so provoking she's unleashed it on you."

"I still don't know what I said that was so awful." He'd spoken the truth about Lord Gilbert. The man *was* reckless, and if he carried on in that unthinking way, it would be only a matter of time before he hurt someone. "You can't deny Gilbert is thoughtless. Or have you forgotten about what happened in the Ring?"

"I'm not arguing the point. It's true that Gilly would do well to pay closer attention to his surroundings. But one might say something true about a person, James, without it being the least bit kind, or helpful."

That was... bloody hell, she was right, wasn't she? Perhaps he had been rather hard on Lord Gilbert, who for all his bumbling, didn't seem to mean any harm. "Yes, very well, but why should Miss Templeton have such a burning desire to champion Gilbert?"

He didn't like it, somehow, that she should be so concerned for him.

"Because no one else is, James. No one who makes any difference, at any rate." She gave him an accusing look. "I daresay she feels a kinship with Lord Gilbert because he's an outcast, in much the same way she and her sisters have always been outcasts."

"Outcasts? Surely, it's not so bad as that? Her sisters are *countesses*."

"I assure you, it *is* that bad. The *ton* has behaved disgracefully towards the Templetons ever since that business with their mother's adulterous affair and the scandal that followed when she fled to the Continent, and it's only grown worse since Euphemia's sisters married. The *ton* is never more vicious than when they're jealous. I can't speak for Gilly, but I know Euphemia often feels very alone when she's in London."

She felt alone? Damn it. That didn't sit well with him. Not at all.

"I didn't mean to upset her." That didn't make his part in this afternoon's scuffle with her any less shameful, however. A proper gentleman didn't drive a lady into a fit of temper.

"I know that, James, yet here we are." She waved a hand toward Miss Templeton, who'd grown smaller with each step across the lawn, until at last, she vanished into a thin copse of trees.

He let out a huff. Squirmed in his chair. Kicked at a rock near the toe of his boot. He knew what he had to do, but—

"James." His aunt laid a hand on his arm. "You really should go and—"

"Yes, I know. I'm going."

"There's a dear boy." She gave his arm a fond pat.

He wandered off in the direction Miss Templeton had gone, composing an apology in his head as he went. He was no good at them, having rarely felt the need to apologize to anyone, for anything.

It was most unpleasant, this feeling of being in the wrong.

He found her seated at the base of a tree, her legs pulled up to her chest. Her arms were wrapped around her knees, and her cheek was resting atop them. To look at her, one would never guess that not ten minutes ago she'd delivered a lecture that made his ears blister. She looked as cool and unruffled as ever, every trace of anger tucked safely away.

"Miss Templeton."

"Lord Fairmont." She blinked up at him, the few rays of afternoon sunlight that had penetrated the canopy of leaves above them falling across her face, and emphasizing the deep blue of her irises.

Her eyes were a very dark blue, just like her sister Tilly's were. He'd never met any of the other three Templeton sisters, but if the gossip was true, their eyes were all the same unusual shade of blue.

He'd never much admired blue eyes, but her eyes were unlike any others he'd ever seen before. So dark, like a summer sky at midnight, with long, thick eyelashes that brushed her cheekbones when she blinked.

Had he ever seen any longer or thicker eyelashes than hers?

If he had, he didn't recall it.

How was it he'd never noticed them before? Had he ever truly looked at Euphemia Templeton before today?

"Miss Templeton," he said again.

"Yes, my lord?"

He paused, studying her, but he couldn't read her expression. Her face was as blank as an untouched artist's canvas.

But she wasn't quite as accomplished at bleeding all the emotion from her tone. He heard the slight quaver in her voice, and all at once the vague sense of regret he'd felt at upsetting her sharpened, digging its claws deep into his chest.

"I, ah... I have a question for you, if you'd agree to indulge me."

She turned toward him, her cheek still resting on her knee, her gaze wary, but after a slight hesitation, she nodded. "Very well."

It was the first time she'd looked directly at him since that strange moment in the Ring, right after the accident with Lord Gilbert, and he took full advantage of it, gazing deeply into her eyes, searching in the depths for the secrets she was hiding.

She hid more than she revealed, but that temper, and her passionate defense of Lord Gilbert... those were real.

Perhaps he should infuriate her more often.

"Am I mistaken, Miss Templeton, in thinking that you just scolded me about my behavior toward Lord Gilbert just now?"

"Me, dare to scold you, my lord? It hardly seems likely, does it?"

Ah, at last, some emotion on that smooth, placid face! How absurd, that he should feel so pleased to be the one to elicit it, but he was like a dog who'd been given a treat for performing a clever trick.

If he'd succeeded once, perhaps he might do so again.

He moved closer, the spreading branches of the elm trees above them whispering in the breeze. "That, Miss Templeton, is not an answer. It's another question."

"Indeed. Any other gentleman might take it as a disinclination on a lady's part to pursue the conversation."

"Now *that* was certainly a scold. That's twice now." It should have irritated him, but instead, an inexplicable urge to laugh swelled in his chest. It was damned odd, given he'd never much enjoyed being scolded before.

"If I did intend it as a scold, Lord Fairmont, I daresay you wouldn't recognize it as one, being the sort of gentleman who is, I can only assume, unused to being scolded."

"Even more reason I *would* recognize it, I'd say."

Her lips twitched. "If you do feel scolded, my lord, perhaps it's less to do with me than with a consciousness on your part of not having behaved precisely as a gentleman ought to have done toward Lord Gilbert."

"Another set down, and so neatly done, Miss Templeton! I begin to quite admire you. That's three times now, and all in less than half an hour. I don't recall ever having been scolded so heartily in my life."

"Yes, well, be that as it may, it's not my place to scold you about anything, is it? I beg your pardon for losing my temper with you, my lord."

"No, don't take it back *now*, Miss Templeton. You were doing so well. I was right on the verge of being properly chastised, I promise you."

"Forgive me, Lord Fairmont, but I don't find this as amusing as you do."

She unwound her arms from around her knees and shifted as if to rise, but he reached out and caught her wrist. "Wait. Please."

She glanced down at his hand, a faint frown line appearing between her brows. "I'm sure Lady Fosberry must be wondering where I am."

"It's alright, Miss Templeton. She sent me to fetch you." He should have released her at once— it's what a gentleman would have done —but instead, he kept ahold of her wrist, the throb of her pulse under the pad of his thumb palpable even through his gloves, and seated himself on the ground beside her. "What, precisely, is your complaint about my treatment of Lord Gilbert? I was perfectly civil to him."

"Civil, yes, but not friendly, my lord."

It *had* been petty of him to leave Gilbert out of the game instead of attempting to rearrange the pairings, but it was as plain as day that Gilbert was developing a *tendre* for Harriett, and he didn't want to encourage it.

Not because of Gilbert's awkward manners, or his questionable taste in clothing, but because he was nearly as naïve and inexperienced as Harriett was. Between the two of them, they were hardly able to tell up from down.

No, a courtship between them was out of the question. When one looked at it rationally, he was doing them a kindness, nipping their infatuation in the bud.

Except it didn't feel like a kindness. It felt like a slight— an undeserved one —and he didn't care for the reflection of himself he saw in Euphemia Templeton's eyes.

"Lord Gilbert is a dear friend of your sister's, my lord. I thought, under the circumstances, that you might exert yourself, but I may be mistaken."

"I wouldn't say that I—"

"Perhaps all that is required of a gentleman these days is cold civility."

"I... that's... I didn't..." But it was no use. Guilty heat was already creeping up the back of his neck.

She was right, damn it. He'd behaved like an arse.

He dragged a hand through his hair, wincing. He didn't care for admitting he was wrong, and he especially didn't care for admitting it to *her*, but he was a gentleman, by God, and a gentleman acknowledged it when he'd made a mistake.

No matter how badly it stung.

"Very well, Miss Templeton. You're right. I admit I might have been a bit more welcoming. I should have been more gracious to Lord Gilbert."

"I'm *right*? You mean to say you're agreeing with me?"

Well, there was no mistaking her expression *now*. Her jaw hung open, and her eyes had gone as wide as saucers.

He huffed out a breath. "For God's sake, Miss Templeton, you needn't look so astonished. Despite what you may think of me, I am capable of admitting it when I'm wrong."

It simply didn't happen often, that was all.

"I don't think of you at all, Lord Fairmont," she said quickly, her chin rising.

"No, of course not." However, if that were the case, would she feel the need to say so? Could it be that she had thought of him, once or twice?

It was an intriguing idea, which was bizarre enough, as he never would have imagined he could ever find anything about Euphemia Templeton intriguing, but here they were, with him gazing down at her, and her gazing up at him as if they'd just seen each other for the first time.

Her eyes were startlingly blue, and her lips the sweetest, softest pink.

They were plumper than one might expect for such a delicate looking lady. Far plumper than they should be. Now he'd noticed it, it was difficult to take his eyes off them, especially now, when she was biting the lower one in such a maddening way, her teeth sinking into the tender flesh, like dollops of cream atop of handful of juicy strawberries.

It seemed incredible he hadn't noticed them before.

Noticed *her*.

But if he had thought her a timid, quiet little mouse, it was because that was the way she wished to be seen.

Or *not* seen. Yes, that was more accurate. If there was a lady more determined to fade into the background than Euphemia Templeton, he'd never encountered her.

But then, perhaps his aunt was right, and she had good reasons for that.

"Before I came in search of you, Miss Templeton, I remarked to my aunt that it surprised me that you should take such an active interest in Lord Gilbert's affairs."

"Oh?" She raised an eyebrow. "I confess I don't see what's so surprising about it. I merely wish to see Lord Gilbert treated with common courtesy. What was Lady Fosberry's reply?"

"She, ah… she didn't venture a guess."

That wasn't the truth, but Miss Templeton had gone tense beside him as soon as he brought it up. No doubt she had her reasons for wishing to protect Gilbert, but she didn't want to share them with him.

"Are you aware, Lord Fairmont, that Viscount Gilbert was raised by his aunt?"

He glanced at her, surprised. "I was not, no."

"Yes. His parents died when he was still an infant. Lady Fosberry tells me his aunt, Miss Gratrakes is a kind, gentle lady, but she's not fashionable and does not spend any time in London. I believe Lord Gilbert had quite an isolated childhood."

"Much like Harriett." It had suited her. Harriett might not be the kind young lady she was if she'd been raised among the *ton*— but for a titled gentleman of means, there were significant drawbacks to such an upbringing.

"I don't deny Lord Gilbert lacks polish, but one can't question the goodness of his heart. He's a generous, sweet-tempered young man." She gave him a long, steady look. "He simply needs a gentleman of sense to set him on the right path."

"I see. What sort of gentleman did you have in mind, Miss Templeton?"

As if he hadn't already guessed.

"Why, a gentleman of sense, taste, and character, Lord Fairmont. A gentleman who behaves as a gentleman ought to behave."

"I hope you don't mean me."

"And if I do, my lord?"

"Then I'll remind you, Miss Templeton, that you've spent half the afternoon scolding me for my deplorable behavior."

"A gentleman with impeccable taste in dress," she went on, ignoring his teasing. "A gentleman, for example, who knows that a navy Weston coat over a navy and gray striped waistcoat, and a handsome pair of top boots are just the thing for an afternoon of playing at bowls."

He glanced down at himself, then back at her with narrowed eyes. "Are you trying to flatter me into doing your bidding, Miss Templeton?"

"Certainly not, Lord Fairmont, although I will

remind you once again that Lord Gilbert has proven himself a faithful friend to your sister."

She gave a sweet smile, as if she hadn't just eviscerated him with the sharp tongue hiding behind those soft, pink lips. "I'll consider it, Miss Templeton. Will that do, or am I to be subjected to another scolding?"

"No, indeed. You'll not hear another word of reproach from my lips, I promise you." She hesitated, her cheeks coloring, then she said in a rush, "Thank you, Lord Fairmont."

"Don't thank me yet, Miss Templeton." He rose, and held out a hand to help her to her feet. "I make no promises where Lord Gilbert is concerned."

But when she took his hand, her dainty fingers curling around his, and her thumb grazing his palm, he knew he was going to do precisely as she asked.

CHAPTER NINE

Viscount Gilbert lived on Lime Street. Lime Street, of all godforsaken places.

Not Albany, Piccadilly, as every fashionable single gentleman of means should do, but Lime Street, and so close to Leadenhall Market, James could hear the squawk of clucking chickens from his place on the doorstep.

If that weren't bad enough, the Spread Eagle Inn, which was just down the street from Gilbert's lodgings, at the corner of Lime and Gracechurch Streets was doing a brisk trade this morning, with people bustling about and delivery wagons coming into and out of the courtyard.

The chickens and the rattle of wagon wheels taken together made such an ungodly racket it was all he could do not to stick his fingers in his ears. How could Gilbert stand it? A man couldn't hear himself think.

Then again, it was Viscount Gilbert. He hadn't seen much evidence thus far that the man spent a significant amount of his time in deep thought. If he had, he'd have known better than to take apartments in Cornhill, of all places.

A gentleman's address was yet another measure by which his peers would judge him, and alas, yet another in which poor Viscount Gilbert fell short.

It made no sense. Gilbert didn't lack the funds for apartments in a more fashionable part of London, so what in the world was he doing *here*? Was it possible Miss Templeton had the right of it, and the viscount simply didn't know the difference between a fashionable address and... here?

One would think the chickens might have given it away.

He knocked briskly on the door, a heavy sigh on his lips. This was all Euphemia Templeton's fault. If she hadn't treated him to the waspish edge of her tongue, it never would have occurred to him to seek Gilbert out at all.

Gilbert, of all people!

He'd been asking himself what he was doing since he'd left his lodgings in St. James's this morning, and he had yet to come up with a satisfactory answer.

One thing, however, was absolutely certain.

His appearance on Gilbert's doorstep didn't have anything to do with that set-down Euphemia Templeton had given him yesterday.

Not a single, blessed thing.

He hadn't spared a thought for Miss Templeton when he'd made his way into the city this morning, nor did he spare her one now as he turned on his heel and made his way back down the steps.

He'd just turn around, return to his lodgings, and forget this nonsense.

But he hadn't even made it as far as the bottom

step before Miss Templeton's voice was echoing in his head, scolding him for his ungentlemanly behavior toward the viscount, her blue eyes spitting fire, and her scolding tongue wriggling like a serpent between those soft, deceptively innocent-looking lips.

Him, ungentlemanly!

Damned if his ears weren't still ringing from that set down she'd given him. He could hardly recall what she'd said now— it was all a blur —but a few things did stand out from the hysterical harangue.

She'd gone on about common courtesy, and then there'd been that business about Gilbert being Harriett's dear friend. She'd even had the gall to imply that James failed to comport himself as a gentleman ought to have done.

Or, well, she hadn't implied it, so much as she'd said it outright.

Miss Templeton, lecturing the Earl of Fairmont about proper gentlemanly behavior!

He paused on the last step, blowing out a breath. The trouble was, Miss Templeton wasn't entirely wrong, damn her.

The truth was that he generally did make a point of being kind to Harriett's friends, and he *had* fallen short when it came to Viscount Gilbert, but this whole business was a great deal more complicated than Miss Templeton realized.

It wasn't that he had anything against Viscount Gilbert. No, not a thing, only—

Oh, very well, damn it, he *did* have something against the viscount. A dozen somethings, starting with that business in the Ring, and ending with the increasingly besotted expression on the man's face whenever he gazed at Harriett.

James had kept a close eye on Gilbert yesterday afternoon after he and Miss Templeton had rejoined the party, and it hadn't taken long to see that things had progressed further than he'd initially thought.

This was no schoolboy's infatuation.

Gilbert fancied himself violently in love with Harriett.

Worse, he'd come to London *for her*.

He spent all his time following Harriett about and making a nuisance of himself, and it was only a matter of time before he begged for her hand in marriage.

As for Harriett's feelings... well, it was difficult to tell with young ladies, but he had an uneasy suspicion that Harriett might return the viscount's affections.

She'd been instantly charmed by him when they'd met at Lord and Lady Houghton's house party in Kent this past summer, and Gilbert had spent every waking moment of the house party following her about like a half-witted schoolboy.

Damn Lord and Lady Houghton, anyway. This was all their fault, for throwing their blasted house party in the first place and inviting such a fool as Viscount Gilbert.

But Harriett didn't think him a fool. Quite the opposite. She couldn't open her mouth these days without going on and on about Lord Gilbert's sweetness, his pleasing temper, and his cleverness.

A cleverness the viscount kept well hidden, by the way.

But Harriett had been equally as enamored of Lord Wyle, hadn't she? She'd found him just as pleasing as she did Gilbert, and look how that had turned out.

Not that he could accuse Gilbert of being the villain Wyle had been. He may not be in favor of a match between Harriett and Gilbert, but even he could see the viscount didn't have a wicked bone in his body.

The trouble with the viscount was that he was flighty and impulsive. Childlike, even, much as Harriett herself was, and the two of them together— good God, it was like pairing a puppy with a newborn kitten.

Gilbert was a bit of a fool, to be honest, and he had no patience for fools.

So, what the devil was he doing here on the man's doorstep?

It had been madness to come here in the first place. He didn't have anything to say to Viscount Gilbert, and God knew his appearance here would only serve to give the viscount hope when he'd much rather not encourage—

"Lord Fairmont?"

Too late, damn it.

Gilbert was standing in the doorway, staring at James, and looking utterly flummoxed to find the Earl of Fairmont on his doorstep.

Well, that made two of them. "Gilbert," he replied curtly, giving the man a brief nod.

Then the two of them stood there like a pair of fools, staring silently at each other, until at last Gilbert gave an awkward little cough, clearing his throat. "How, er, how do you do, my lord?"

James wasn't in the mood for trivial pleasantries, and given the squealing chickens and the dust from the wagon wheels besmirching his new Hoby boots, it was a question that was far better left unanswered.

So he didn't answer, but instead got straight to the heart of the thing. "Do you plan to attend Lord Powell's ball tomorrow night?"

Gilbert's eyebrows shot up. "Er, yes?"

"Is that an answer, Gilbert, or another question? I couldn't tell."

"Yes, Lord Fairmont. I do plan to attend."

"Do you intend to ask my sister to dance?"

"Er, well, I did have hopes of—"

"Yes, or no, Gilbert?" God above, it was like pulling teeth.

Or beheading chickens.

"Yes." Gilbert huffed, crossing his arms over his chest. "I intend to ask Lady Harriett to dance, not that it's any concern of—"

"Mine? Of course, it's my concern. I *am* her brother."

Gilbert swallowed. "Of course, my lord. I beg your pardon."

"Yes, yes, it's fine." It wasn't fine, not really, but there was no question that Harriett would accept Gilbert's invitation to dance, so the only thing to do now was make certain the man didn't make a spectacle of both of them. "Lord Powell is a fashionable gentleman, and his ball is certain to be the height of elegance. Do you have the proper attire for the evening?"

"I believe my clothing to be perfectly acceptable—"

"Show me."

Gilbert blinked. "You want me to *show you* the clothing I intend to wear to Lord Powell's ball?"

It was, admittedly, a trifle unusual for a gentleman to appear uninvited on another gentleman's doorstep and demand to see his wardrobe, but it was Gilbert's own fault for appearing in that dreadful canary yellow coat in the Ring the other day, and that was to say nothing of that sky blue monstrosity he'd worn yesterday. "Yes, Gilbert, I do."

Gilbert's eyebrows lowered in a scowl, his cheeks flushing with the first hint of temper James had ever seen from him. Ah, so the man did have some pride, after all.

"You have a bloody nerve, Fairmont, showing up here and—"

"That's the spirit, Gilbert. I was beginning to wonder if you had it in you."

Gilbert's jaw fell open. "Christ, Fairmont. You're mad, you know that?"

Not yet, no, but he likely would be before the season was over and Harriett was safely wed. "Yes, yes, it's all very shocking. Now, are you going to invite me in, or not?"

Gilbert glared at him, but then he shrugged, opened the door wider, and stood back. "I suppose I have to, now that you're here."

He did, indeed, and James would have to accept, and God knew what further ridiculousness this would lead to, but he loved Harriett dearly, and if Viscount Gilbert was the only gentleman who would make her happy, then...

So be it.

At least Euphemia Templeton would be pleased.

Not that he'd done it to please *her*. Not at all.

Another sigh escaped him as he mounted the steps and followed Gilbert into a rather dark, cramped hallway, his nose wrinkling. "What is that ungodly smell?"

Gilbert sniffed. "The wind must be coming from the east today."

"The wind? What does the bloody wind have to do with anything?"

"There's a fishmonger's just down the road." Gilbert closed the door, and made his way down the hallway, gesturing to James to follow him.

James reached into his pocket, withdrew his handkerchief, and pressed it to his nose. "Of course, there is."

"WHAT DO you think of this ribbon, Euphemia?" Lady Fosberry selected a length of midnight blue velvet ribbon from the selection spread out on the glass counter of Madame Dubois' shop, and turned to Phee.

"Oh, it's so pretty!" Harriett caught the ribbon and brought it to Phee, who'd exhausted the last of her patience for ribbons and laces, and taken a seat on a bench by the window overlooking Bond Street. "What a delightful blue! It's the perfect color."

"It is very pretty." Phee traced her thumb over the nap, which was as soft as a rose petal under her touch. "Very fine, too, but I thought you were wearing your green silk to Lord Powell's ball. I don't think you want blue ribbons with it, do you?"

"My dearest Euphemia, it's not for Harriett, but for you." Lady Fosberry marched across the shop and took the seat beside her on the bench. "Before Mathilda left for Oxfordshire, she gave you that di-

vine blue silk and velvet ballgown. It's the ideal gar-
ment for the ball. I thought we might persuade you to
wear it."

Her, dressed up in velvet and silk? No, indeed. "I
don't think—"

"Yes, you must wear it, Phee!" Harriett cried.
"You'll look positively smashing in that shade of
blue!"

Smashing? Tilly's blue silk ballgown had been
made for a countess. It was much too grand for the
likes of her. She'd look like an utter fool wearing it,
like a spinster playing at being an aristocrat, and the
ton would laugh themselves sick. "I thought I'd wear
my embroidered brown muslin—"

"Goodness, no!" Lady Fosberry gasped. "My
dearest Euphemia, you cannot wear *muslin* to Lord
Powell's ball."

"Certainly not, and that shade of brown isn't
fashionable this season." Harriett frowned at her.
"Come now, Phee. There's no need for you to dress as
if you're an aged spinster."

"But I *am* a spinster, Harriett. There's no use pre-
tending otherwise, and anyway, I'm not ashamed of
it." Not at all, although there was no denying the
word spinster was an unpleasant one, and stung her
tongue a bit on the way out of her mouth.

"For pity's sake, you're only twenty-four years
old! That's hardly ancient. Please, Phee." Harriett
caught her hand. "I want you to dance, and enjoy
yourself."

Dance? Dear God, what a terrifying prospect
that was.

She much preferred to remain on the sidelines
and meld seamlessly into the background, but Har-

riett looked so earnest, so hopeful, she couldn't bring herself to disappoint her. "Very well, if you feel that strongly about it, I'll wear the blue gown, although I daresay I won't have a surplus of dancing partners, no matter what I—"

"James!" Harriett exclaimed.

Who, Lord Fairmont? Why, what could Harriett mean? Of all the gentlemen in London, he was the last one who'd wish to dance with *her*. Which was just as well, of course, because she certainly didn't want to dance with *him*. The two of them could hardly look at each other without one of them falling into a temper. "I would be exceedingly surprised, Harriett, if your brother invited me to dance."

"Dance? Oh no, I meant James is here." Harriett nodded toward the window. "Just there, on the pavement outside, and what do you think? He's with Gilly!"

"*Here*?" Phee whirled back toward the window so quickly, she nearly smacked her forehead against the glass.

There, on the other side of Madame Dubois's wide window was Lord Fairmont, looking smart, indeed, in a navy coat fitted to such perfection it lay perfectly smooth over his shoulders, a narrow strip of brocaded waistcoat in a muted green stripe visible at his waist, and every silky strand of his dark hair in place.

A sigh— a most humiliatingly wistful sigh —escaped her before she could smother it. Lord Fairmont was the most insufferably arrogant man she'd ever come across, but there was no denying he was, head to toe, the vision of a fashionable aristocratic gentleman.

At least, until he opened his mouth.

Still, every time she encountered him, he looked nothing less than resplendent.

"He's so handsome!" Harriett crowded onto the bench, pressing her nose to the glass. "Isn't he handsome, Phee?"

"Er, well..." Lord Fairmont was, of course, terribly handsome, but once she admitted it aloud, she'd no longer be able to pretend it wasn't true. "Handsomeness is a matter of opinion, not—"

Harriett interrupted with a yearning sigh of her own. "He looks very well in his mauve coat, does he not? It's not the usual color for a gentleman's coat, but I think it suits him."

Mauve coat? What mauve... oh! She was referring to Gilly, not her brother who wouldn't be caught even in his coffin outfitted in a mauve-colored coat. She'd wager every penny in her reticule on it. "It's, ah, a lovely color, yes."

Beside her, Lady Fosberry smothered a snort. "You look surprised, Euphemia. One might almost conclude you were gazing at someone else?"

Phee cast her a withering look. "I wasn't looking at anyone at all, I assure you."

Fortunately, Harriett didn't notice this exchange, as she had eyes only for Gilly. Eyes, and knuckles, because before Phee could stop her, Harriett reached over and gave the window a sharp rap. "Harriett, for pity's sake!"

But it was too late. Both gentlemen turned. As soon as Gilly spied Harriett on the other side of the glass his face lit up with a smile.

At least, she thought it did. She only glimpsed it in her peripheral vision, because Lord Fairmont's gaze caught hers as soon as he turned, and once it did, she couldn't look away.

Neither, it seemed, could he. They both stilled, staring at each other through the glass.

One moment passed, then another, then a hundred moments, or it felt that way to her, time spooling out in an endless thread, his dark eyes holding hers for so long her cheeks began to burn, and the corners of her lips to twitch, as if a smile would have its way with them whether she approved it or not, and then...

All at once, Lord Fairmont swept his hat from his head and offered her a bow so deep, and with such an exaggerated flourish that it could only have been meant mockingly.

Incorrigible man!

She turned around with a huff and faced forward again, her cheeks still burning.

"My, how fascinating," Lady Fosberry murmured.

Phee turned to her. "What? What's fascinating?"

Lady Fosberry was watching her, a speculative look in her eyes. "Why, you and James, of course."

Phee drew herself up with a sniff. "Nonsense. There's not a single thing I find fascinating about Lord Fairmont, I assure you."

"Indeed? Well, he doesn't seem to feel the same way about you." Lady Fosberry nodded toward the window. "He's still staring at you."

She *wasn't* going to look. No, not a single glance, dash it. Lord Fairmont could save his mocking smiles for someone who appreciated—

The bell above the shop door tinkled, and boot-steps crossed the wooden floor, stopping in front of her. They were exceptionally fine boots— black, and cut high, to just under the knee, and set off to perfection by a pair of tight, buff-colored pantaloons.

"Miss Templeton."

Goodness, the man was everywhere, it seemed. She let out a sigh, but there was no avoiding it, so she raised her gaze to his face, and, dash it, there went her lips again, curling upwards of their own accord. "Lord Fairmont."

"What luck, that we should run into you. I daresay you're shopping for Lord Powell's ball. Will you show me your purchases, Miss Templeton?"

"You'll have to excuse me, Lord Fairmont. I haven't made any purchases."

"What, you've come all the way to Bond Street, and haven't made a single purchase? I don't believe it."

My, he was enjoying himself, wasn't he? "I do hate to disappoint you, my lord, but—"

"Oh, but Phee, you've promised you'll have these blue ribbons." Harriett tugged on one end of the ribbons in Phee's hand. "You'd better take them now, because I saw Lady Henry eyeing them."

"Blue ribbons? How shocking." Lord Fairmont's lips twitched as he gazed down at her, his eyes twinkling. "Were they out of gray ribbons, Miss Templeton?"

"Gray!" Harriett repeated. "Don't be ridiculous, James. Who wants gray ribbons? No one wears *gray* to a ball."

"No? I'm enormously relieved to hear it. These blue ribbons are very pretty. Dare I hope, Miss Templeton, that you intend to wear midnight blue to Lord Powell's ball?"

"I-I haven't yet made up my mind what—"

"She does, indeed!" Harriett clapped her hands. "A beautiful midnight blue velvet and silk. I can't wait to see you in it, Phee. I'm certain you'll look like an angel."

With that, Harriett pushed the ribbons into Phee's hand, then rushed off to join Gilly at the counter.

"May I see them?" Lord Fairmont held out his hand.

She glanced at Harriett's retreating back, then down at the ribbons clutched in her fist, and at the glossy toes of Lord Fairmont's boots— anywhere, but at his face, because —oh, it was absurd, but she didn't want to show the ribbons to him, because...

They were too much for her, too colorful, and somehow, they made her ashamed.

"Miss Templeton." His voice was soft. "Show me the ribbons."

She could hardly refuse, could she? Indeed, she was being ridiculous.

So, she held out her hand. He plucked them from her fingers and ran his thumb over them. "The color," he murmured after a moment. "I think they're..." He held the ribbons up to her face, close to her cheek. "Yes. They're the exact same shade of blue as your eyes."

Was he poking fun at her? She glanced up at him from under her lashes, half-dreading what she'd find in that sharp gaze.

But there was nothing ugly there, nothing mocking.

What she did see there made her catch her breath.

"An angel, indeed." He closed his fingers around her wrist, drew her hand toward him, and pressed the blue ribbons into her palm. "An angel, with midnight blue eyes."

Then he was gone, the bell on the shop door tinkling as he went out, leaving her gazing after him as he made his way down Bond Street, a handful of blue silk ribbons caught in her fist.

ANNA BRADLEY

CHAPTER
TEN

I t had been a mistake, wearing Tilly's blue silk and velvet ballgown tonight.

The midnight blue ribbons, the sapphire and diamond ear bobs Harriett had lent her, the elegant chignon it had taken an hour to perfect...

Mistakes, each and every one of them.

Terrible, drastic mistakes.

Phee didn't reach this conclusion until she, Lady Fosberry, and Harriett arrived at Lord Powell's ball, and by then, it was too late.

Half a dozen steps was all it took. She hadn't ventured more than half a dozen steps into the ballroom before the enormity of these blunders crashed down upon her like an overturned carriage.

It wasn't that the gown didn't suit her. It was that it *did*.

The cut of the bodice, the way the silk clung to her curves, and the deep, midnight blue velvet overskirt, with the matching blue ribbons in her hair— her looking glass had plainly told her whatever modest claims she'd once had to beauty hadn't entirely deserted her.

She'd never been one to linger at her toilette, or waste time admiring her own reflection, but tonight, when she'd looked in the glass, she hadn't seen a spinster staring back at her.

Tonight, she'd discovered the version of herself she'd thought gone forever— a young lady with bright eyes and flushed cheeks, who was about to attend her very first ball, in her very first London season.

Her first, and last.

Of course, she hadn't known it then.

No, she'd been as eager as every other young lady that night as she twirled in front of the glass and imagined how many times she might dance that evening, and with whom, her head filled with romantic notions about the delicious ways in which her season might unfold.

It felt like a lifetime ago, but tonight, when she'd stood in front of the glass staring at her reflection, toying with a fold of the rich velvet overskirt, that young, hopeful version of herself had been there as if she'd been waiting for the past six years for Phee to find her again.

To find herself.

So soft, that velvet skirt. Had she ever felt anything as soft? And the silk, too, so thin, so fine and delicate it was like a puff of warm breath over her skin, like a whisper from a lover's lips.

Her lady's maid had taken special care with her hair tonight, as well. It was brown— not as dark a brown as Juliet's, nor as light as Emmeline's —but a plain, dull brown, indistinguishable from every other shade of plain, dull brown.

At least, that was how she'd always seen it, but

tonight it had been brushed until it gleamed a rich mahogany, and her lady's maid had woven the blue ribbon Harriett had chosen for her into the locks and finished it with a dozen or so pearl-tipped hairpins scattered among the waves.

As she'd gazed at her reflection tonight, it had felt almost as if she'd somehow stepped back in time, to when she'd been young and full of hope, and for an instant— just a single, fleeting instant— she'd felt like the young girl she'd once been.

The feeling had lasted as she'd made her way down the staircase at Fosberry house and throughout the drive to Lord Powell's townhouse in Grosvenor Square. It had stayed with her until she'd stepped into the ballroom, and she, Harriett, and Lady Fosberry began to make their way toward Lady Powell, who was holding court on the opposite side of the ballroom.

Half a dozen steps, before she wished for the floor to open up beneath her and swallow her whole.

It began with the stares. Dozens of narrowed eyes followed her progress, the weight of them growing heavier with every step she took. Then the whispers, which gave way to smirks soon enough, then titters half-smothered behind fans and gloved hands.

She couldn't hear what they said, but it didn't matter. She could imagine it.

Putting on airs... the gown far too grand for her humble station in life... seeking attention, as the Templeton sisters always did, never happy until they'd drawn every eye to them...

A spinster, playing at dress up.

Every muscle in her body tensed, every instinct urging her to run back out the way she'd come, and never attend another ball again, but before she could flee, Lady Fosberry's gloved hand landed on her wrist. "Don't listen to a word of it, Euphemia. Not a single word, my dearest girl. You look positively ravishing this evening."

"You do, Phee." Harriett took her other arm and drew it through hers, scowling at a smirking Lady Arundel as they passed. "You're beautiful. That shade of blue is a perfect match for your eyes! Why, that gown was made for you. Don't pay any attention to them. They're just bitter, jealous old witches."

"I... thank you." She smiled at Harriett and squeezed Lady Fosberry's hand.

Her friends were utterly sincere— she only had to look into their eyes to see that— but her own joy in her appearance had vanished by then, and all she wanted, all she wished for in the world was that she'd worn one of her somber brown or dark green ball gowns, so she might fade into the background as she always did.

Or better yet, that she'd never come here at all.

She managed to keep her head high as she crossed the ballroom, and she managed to paste a sickly smile to her lips as they paid their compliments to Lady Powell, but the whispers and muffled laughter seemed to swell around her, growing louder with every moment that passed until her head seemed to vibrate with the deafening echo inside her skull.

"Phee?" Harriett squeezed her hand. "Are you alright? You're very pale."

"Yes, I... I'm..." Harriett's face swam before her eyes.

Everyone was staring at her. Staring, and laughing.

How had she ever imagined a drive in the Ring was more torturous than a ballroom? At least on the promenade, she was partially shielded from prying eyes by the carriage. Surely, there must be an alcove she could duck into or a corner around which she could disappear—

"Good evening, Miss Templeton."

She started as if she'd been stung, the low, rich voice jerking her loose from the fog in her head, and gazed up into blue eyes that had somehow, against her every effort, become nearly as familiar to her as her own.

When had that happened? Why hadn't she taken better care to guard against it? "Lord Fairmont. I... how do you do?"

He didn't answer. He didn't even appear to hear her, so absorbed was he in studying her.

He took in the ribbons woven into her hair, and the pendant around her neck. He lingered at the pearl nestled in the hollow of her throat before moving lower, his eyes warm as he took in the tight bodice of her gown, her full silk skirts, and the tips of the toes of her satin slippers peeking out from under her hems.

He was silent for some time after he finished his perusal, but at last, he let out a soft, "Hmmm."

Hmmm? What in the world did that mean?

But she knew, already. Of course, she knew. He thought her as ridiculous as every other fashionable aristocrat, in her borrowed finery. It was hardly a surprise, yet somehow, it hurt more than any of the other snickers or mocking sidelong glances she'd received this evening.

"Finally," he murmured. "It's well past time, Miss Templeton."

She didn't want to know what he meant. She couldn't bear a jibe from him right now, but her traitorous mouth was already opening, her jaw unhinging with a rusty squeak, words heavy with defiance and shame crowding onto the end of her tongue. "Well past time for what?"

"It's well past time you stopped dressing as if you're an aged spinster."

She stared up at him, a flash of heat scorching her cheeks even as a chill rushed over her, tugging goosebumps to the surface of her skin.

She *was* an aged spinster. A spinster, dressed in a countess's ballgown.

"I... forgive me, my lord, but I can't... I'm in need of the ladies' retiring room."

Lord Fairmont blinked down at her, a frown gathering between his brows. He opened his mouth to speak, but Harriett interrupted him, seizing her hand. "You can't go now, Phee! We've only just arrived, and look! Lord Hemming is coming our way!"

Lord Hemming? Did she know Lord Hemming? She glanced up, but the ballroom was a sea of blurred faces, none of them at all familiar to her.

"He's looking right at you, Phee," Harriett breathed. "I daresay he's going to ask you to dance!"

Dance? Oh, no. No. Every eye would be upon her then.

"No, I... no, thank you. I beg your pardon, but I..." She tugged loose from Harriett's grip and began to back away from them.

"Miss Templeton." Lord Fairmont stepped toward her, and a pair of warm, strong hands wrapped around her upper arms, halting her in her place. "Are you unwell?"

"Wait, Euphemia." Lady Fosberry reached out a hand to her, but Phee whirled around before her ladyship could stop her, and ran back in the direction she'd come, eyes following her as she flew past, her skirts clutched in her hands, and rushed toward... where?

Oh, where was the ladies' retiring room?

She couldn't remember, couldn't *think*.

But she ran blindly on, through the ballroom, past the staring eyes and grinning mouths, not caring where she was going, as long as it was away from here.

Because that young lady she'd once been, with eyes full of hope, no longer existed. Because she could never be that young lady again. She couldn't go back in time, no matter how much she might wish she could. Because the reflection she'd seen in the looking glass tonight was a lie.

And because she was a coward. Deep down, she'd always been a coward.

"WHAT THE DEVIL JUST HAPPENED?" James glanced from his aunt to his sister, then back toward the streak of blue silk that was Miss Templeton, tearing across the ballroom like a runaway horse.

"They're laughing at her," Harriett hissed, her face white with rage.

"Who?" Who was laughing, and at whom? None of this made any sense.

"The *ton* is laughing at Euphemia," his aunt said.

"The worst of them, at any rate. Those who aren't laughing at her are whispering and staring."

"But *why*?" What was there to laugh at? She was utter perfection in her blue gown, so lovely his breath had actually caught when he'd glimpsed her across the ballroom. "She looks beautiful this evening."

His aunt let out a sigh. "That's precisely why, James."

"London is overflowing with jealous old harridans who despise the Templetons." Harriett's hands were clenched into fists. "Phee's sisters each stole an eligible earl out from under the *ton*'s noses, and they're determined to keep Phee in her place before she does the same."

That was... God above, it was the most ridiculous thing he'd ever heard. He'd never had much patience for the *ton*— they were idle at best, and at worst, vindictive and spiteful —but this was beyond anything. For the first time, he began to understand what it was costing Miss Templeton to remain in London.

He turned to his aunt. "Is it really as bad as that?"

"I'm afraid so, James." His aunt shook her head. "I should have known this would happen when I saw her in that gown. Perhaps we were wrong, Harriett, in encouraging her to wear it?"

"*What*? For God's sake, no!" His voice was louder than he'd intended, and several people turned to stare at them, but damn it, this was the first time he'd ever seen Euphemia Templeton in a gown that did her justice. "It's absurd, that such a lovely young lady should be dressed as if she's in her dotage."

Harriett raised an eyebrow. "Do you think her lovely, James?"

"She... I...." Did he think her lovely? He hadn't

used to think so— he hadn't *used* to think of her at all — but that was before he'd truly looked at her, before he'd seen underneath the disguises she wore.

The plain gray gowns, the retiring air, the downcast eyes.

That was before he'd seen *her*.

Now... well, he was far from indifferent to her, and what was even more absurd was that it was all because of that blistering scold she'd given him at bowls the other day.

It was pathetic, really.

But he wasn't going to explain it to Harriett, so he said only, "She's well enough. But why did she run away? I meant to pay her a compliment, not insult her."

Although it hadn't been much of a compliment, had it? A gentleman who truly wished to express his admiration to a lady generally kept away from phrases like "aging spinster."

Damn it. He'd made a mess of it. He'd hurt her feelings—

"You don't understand her dread of being ridiculed, James," his aunt said. "Euphemia has her reasons, I assure you, but it's too complicated a story to delve into now. Would you go and find her, Harriett? She needn't return to the ballroom if she doesn't wish to, but I don't like her being off alone right now."

"I'll go."

"*You?*" His aunt repeated, astonished. Both she and Harriett were gaping at him like a pair of fish with hooks in their mouths, but he didn't pause to explain himself or entertain any objections.

He turned on his heel and strode off in the direction Miss Templeton had gone, and his expression must have been fierce, indeed, because no one attempted to stop him. They all scurried out of his way like a pack of mindless sheep as he stormed through.

It took a devil of a time to find her. He waited outside the ladies' retiring room for ages until he finally asked one of the footmen if he'd seen a lady in a blue gown, and the man directed him to a small courtyard down at the end of an adjacent hallway, off the music room.

She was there, perched on the edge of a stone fountain. She didn't look up when he approached, and he didn't speak, either, but sat down beside her, waiting.

She'd been dangling her fingers in the basin of the fountain, and watching the water drops fall from her fingertips, but now she shook them off and turned to face him, and her eyes were so dark with shadows, they looked like bruises in her pale face. "That was silly of me, fleeing the ballroom like a frightened mouse, wasn't it?"

"Was that what happened? I thought there must have been a fire I was unaware of."

It was, thank God, the right thing to say, because after one frozen instant her shoulders relaxed, and a soft chuckle left her lips. "No, just a shamefully spineless lady."

Spineless? Was that how she saw herself? "I hope you aren't referring to yourself. You're many things, Miss Templeton, but you're far from spineless."

"I just fled the entire length of a ballroom because people whose opinions I should care nothing about were staring at me. I'd call that spineless."

Except they hadn't just been staring. They'd been

whispering and smirking and laughing, as well. "I suppose you could have told them all to go to the devil. You didn't hesitate to unleash that sharp tongue of yours on me the other day, so why not the snickering *ton*?"

"I scolded you on Lord Gilbert's behalf." She dropped her gaze, staring down at her hands. "I've, ah... I've never been quite as brave at defending myself."

"It is harder to speak up in one's own defense, yes." Particularly if one didn't believe they deserved defending. Was that the case with Euphemia Templeton? Did she imagine that she somehow deserved the *ton*'s scorn, because she'd championed her younger sisters' right to marry whom they chose?

He studied her profile— the elegant cheekbones, the hint of stubbornness in her jaw, the moonlight toying with the dark locks of her hair, and all at once the one thing he wanted more than anything else was to take back the comment he'd made to her in the ballroom and replace it with something else.

Something true.

That she looked beautiful tonight. That he'd never seen anything as lovely as her in that gown, with her midnight blue ribbons in her hair. That she was no coward.

But all he said was, "It's a shame you left the ballroom. I intended to invite you to waltz."

She cast him a glance from under her lashes. "That's kind of you, my lord, but I... I don't think I'll return to the ballroom tonight."

He wanted to argue with her, but he didn't. Instead, he rose to his feet. "I'll escort you back to Fosberry House, then."

She glanced up at him, her eyes wide. "Oh, I couldn't ask you to do that, Lord Fairmont."

"You didn't ask me, Miss Templeton. I offered. Come." He held out his arm. "I'll return to the ballroom and tell my aunt and Harriett you're unwell, and then I'll take you home."

CHAPTER
ELEVEN

J ames had intended to return to his lodgings in St. James after he took Euphemia home, but instead, he ended up wandering around Fosberry House, fragmented images from the evening muddling his head.

Like the way his heart had quickened when he'd seen Euphemia enter the ballroom, a dazzling vision in midnight blue. Then her face, not ten minutes later, eyes downcast and cheeks scarlet with humiliation as she fled the ballroom, and the defeated slump of her shoulders as she sat at the edge of the fountain, drops of water falling from her fingertips.

What was he meant to do with himself, after such an evening as that?

Nothing felt right to him now.

Eventually, he found his way to the study, and that was where Harriett found him several hours later. "I suppose Phee's gone off to bed?" she asked, leaning a shoulder against the door frame.

"As soon as we returned home, yes." She'd disappeared up the stairs as if she believed she could outrun her demons if only she ran quickly enough.

"The *ton chased* her out of the ballroom tonight, James. It couldn't have been any worse if they'd been wielding torches and pitchforks."

"If I hadn't seen it with my own eyes, I wouldn't have believed it possible." There were a dozen different reasons to despise the *ton*— their avarice, their heartlessness —but he'd never imagined even the worst among them could behave with such cruelty.

Harriett crossed the room and dropped into the chair across from him with a sigh. "I don't suppose we'll ever get Phee to attend another ball, after tonight."

He'd been staring into the fire, watching the flames dance in the grate, but now he looked up. "She must, Harriett. She can't run from them forever."

Then again, perhaps she could. Once this season was over, she had no reason to ever return to London again, if she didn't wish to.

If Euphemia had only been running from the *ton*, it might be just as well, but she wasn't.

She was running from herself, too.

And that... no, that wouldn't do.

"But what's to be done, James?" Harriett spread her hands. "Lady Upton's ball is the week after next. It would do her a world of good to attend, and face them all with her head held high, but it's not as if we can drag her there."

"No, she's much too stubborn for that." It made no sense that such a strong-minded lady should be so intimidated by the *ton*. "I don't understand it, Harriet. Euphemia Templeton has a tongue like a rapier. Why doesn't she wield it against the *ton*, instead of running away from them?"

"It's more complicated than you imagine, James. Phee is protective of those she loves and fierce in her defense of them. I witnessed her deliver a grand set down once when Lady Clyde made a disparaging remark about her sister Emmeline. It was glorious." Harriett grinned, recalling it, but then her smile faded. "But it's not so easy to defend oneself, I suppose."

"Not always, no." Euphemia had said something similar to him tonight herself. "I'd thought to dance a waltz with her tonight," he murmured, more to himself than Harriett.

"I would have liked to have seen that." Harriett paused, considering. "Although now you say it, I don't believe Phee knows how to waltz."

"What? How can she not know how to waltz?" Didn't every young lady in England know how to waltz?

"You forget, James, that Phee's season took place six years ago before the waltz became the rage. They didn't even allow it at Almack's back then. It was considered improper."

He stared at her. "Do you mean to say Euphemia Templeton hasn't danced in *six years*?" That was impossible.

"Not much, no. She usually declines to dance at balls, although she did dance with Mr. Darby last season, but I believe it was quadrille, not a waltz."

Good Lord, could it really be the case that Euphemia didn't know how to waltz? That was... no, that wouldn't do. Not at all.

"I'm going to go peek in on Phee, and then I'm off to bed." Harriett gave a great yawn as she rose to her feet, but she paused at the door before going out.

"Gilly tells me the two of you have plans to have a ride together this week, James."

"Yes. The day after tomorrow. I hope he rides better than he drives. He does know how to properly sit a saddle, doesn't he?" He smiled to take the sting out of his words.

"He does, indeed." Harriett studied him for an instant. "It's kind of you to spend time with him. He doesn't know many gentlemen in London— at least, not many worthy ones, and he's... well, I'm grateful to you."

"It's not me you should thank, Harriett, but Miss Templeton. It's all her doing. She scolded me into it." He'd been mightily affronted by it at the time, but now he'd begun to think she'd done him a great favor.

Somehow, in the upheaval of their parents' deaths, his inheriting an impoverished earldom, and leaving England, he'd forgotten how to be kind.

He'd lost a vital part of himself, and she... she'd helped him to find it again. What more could a man ask, than a lady who reminded him how to be the best version of himself?

Such a lady as that was rare, and she was a gift.

"That does sound like Phee." Harriett stood in the doorway, staring at him. At one point she started to speak, but then subsided, wringing her hands.

Ah. They'd come to it, at last. Even after their years apart, he could still see her thoughts on her face as clearly as if she'd spoken them aloud. Well then, he'd have to help her a bit, wouldn't he?

He cleared his throat. "I take it, Harriett, that you're rather fond of Lord Gilbert."

The sudden surge of color in her cheeks was answer enough. "Er, yes. I am."

James studied the tip of his shoe, hiding his smile. "Perhaps you're a bit *more* than just fond of him?"

She went still. "I— perhaps I am, yes."

"I see. Well then, I suppose Farthingale is out."

She rolled her eyes. "He was never *in*, James."

"No, I suppose not. A pity, really, although I admit Lord Gilbert— *Gilly*, if I must —isn't quite the fool I initially thought him to be. His clothing leaves a great deal to be desired, of course, and he has no business driving a phaeton until he's had proper lessons, but..."

"But?"

"But if he *were* to ever work up the nerve to ask me for your hand, I wouldn't refuse him."

"Oh, thank you, James!" Harriett rushed across the room, threw her arms around his neck, and pressed a kiss to his cheek, just as she'd used to do when she was a child, and he'd soothed one of her hurts.

It was different between them now, of course. It wouldn't ever be the same as it once had been, but it wasn't meant to be, and this... well, this would do.

Yes, he could get used to this. It was rather nice, really, having a grown-up sister.

He pressed a kiss to her forehead. "I've only ever wanted your happiness, Hattie."

"I know. I've always known that, even when I was angry with you. You really are the most excellent brother, James."

"I am, indeed." He gave her an awkward pat. "Now, off to bed with you."

"Yes, alright. Goodnight, James."

"'Night, Hattie."

It was time he went to his own bed, but he remained where he was for some time, staring into the fire until it burned down to the embers, and thinking about blue eyes, water droplets falling from fingertips, and ladies who'd never learned to waltz.

~

"Are you certain I can't assist you with anything, my lord?"

James turned away from the staircase, biting back an irritable grunt. That was the third time Watkins had asked him that question, and the butler was watching him as if he were a thief with his eye on the silver teaspoons.

He'd come downstairs disgracefully early this morning. Now he was pacing from one end of the entryway to the other, and whirling toward the staircase at the slightest sound from above— the squeak of a floorboard, or the echo of footsteps in the corridor.

To an uninformed observer, he might appear a trifle suspicious.

Perhaps he should have waited outside Euphemia's bedchamber door, instead of lingering in the entryway, but it had seemed a bit, er... predatory to pounce upon a lady as soon as she ventured a toe outside her bedchamber.

It wasn't as if he were *stalking* her.

He simply wished to keep his personal matters private, that was all, and that meant not waking either his aunt or his sister. They always slept late in the morning after a ball. As long as they weren't disturbed, they wouldn't be downstairs for hours yet.

Which was precisely what he wanted. If either of

them knew what he was about, he'd never hear the bloody end of it.

And it wasn't as if it *meant* anything.

A gentleman might do a lady a good turn without it meaning a single, blessed thing, but there was no sense in trying to persuade Harriett or his aunt of that. They'd immediately assume he was enamored of Miss Templeton, and then he'd never have another moment of peace.

Him, enamored of Euphemia Templeton. The very idea was absurd. He was no more enamored of her than a schoolboy was of his headmaster.

Which was to say, not at all enamored.

At best, he and Miss Templeton tolerated each other. At their worst, they were like two enraged cats trapped together in a burlap sack, hissing and clawing at each other.

What, then, did he think he was doing? Euphemia Templeton wasn't any concern of his.

It didn't make any sense that he'd been awake for the better part of last night, haunted by the expression on her face when she'd fled the ballroom, the mocking laughter of the *ton* in her wake.

It was just that she'd looked so... desolate, so defeated, her blue eyes full of dark shadows. The *ton* didn't make it easy for her to be in London. From what Harriett and his aunt had told him, they hadn't made it easy for any of the Templeton sisters, but her younger sisters were all countesses now. They had husbands to defend them from the sharpest cuts of the gossips' razored tongues.

Euphemia didn't have anyone, aside from his aunt and his sister.

Bad odds, that. Not at all sporting.

It couldn't be pleasant for her to have to overhear their whispers or see their sneering faces, yet she'd come to London to help Harriett, all the same.

Which was excessively foolish of her, of course. Harriett didn't need her help. Miss Templeton would much better have stayed home, but she was here now, and he... well, he could spare part of his morning for a lady who'd sacrificed months of her time, as well as her peace of mind to help his sister.

But it didn't mean anything. Of course, it didn't. It meant less than nothing.

He resumed his pacing— back and forth, the weight of Watkins' increasingly baffled gaze following his progress, the tap of his boots against the marble floors far louder than they should be, louder than they'd ever been before, as if a bloody horse were galloping from one end of the entryway to the other.

"You're quite certain I can't assist you, Lord Fairmont?"

God above, but the man was persistent. "Yes, yes, I'm perfectly sure, Watkins, but perhaps I'll just go and wait in the library."

"Very good, my lord."

He marched to the end of the corridor and went into the library, but he didn't take a seat. Instead, he waited by the door, on alert for the sound of footsteps. Miss Templeton was fond of reading, and would come this way sooner or later.

Not that he was skulking. It was nothing so devious as that. He was just... lurking around the corner, waiting for her to appear.

What in the world was keeping her?

The timing was perfect. Now, if the lady would

only see fit to venture from her bedchamber, he could get on with his—

"Good morning, Watkins."

He stilled, listening.

"Good morning, Miss Templeton."

Ah, at last!

He waited, ears perked for the sound of footsteps coming down the hallway, but he didn't hear a thing. Had she gone the other way, toward the breakfast room?

He was just about to risk a quick peek around the edge of the library door when he heard the soft rustle of a lady's skirts, then the faint shuffle of footsteps against the thickly carpeted hallway.

Closer, then closer still, another few steps, and...

He ducked back behind the door. An instant later she slipped into the library, and made her way to a chair on one side of the glass doors that led to the terrace, throwing herself into it with the abandon of a lady who believed herself to be alone.

"Now, where did I put..." She rummaged through the cushions and pulled a small book out of its hiding place. "Ah, ha. There you are."

She flipped the pages until she'd found her place, then wriggled about in the chair, leaning her head against one arm and throwing her legs over the other, her somber gray skirts trailing on the floor.

So, she was back to the drab, dull colors, was she? No more silk and velvet for Miss Templeton, it seemed, and no more midnight blue ribbons. After last night, she was back to attempting to hide in plain sight.

He couldn't blame her, really, but it was a wasted effort. She was good at making herself invisible, yes, but once a man did take notice of her, there wasn't a gown gray enough to hide her.

Now he'd seen her, he couldn't *unsee* her.

There was something about her features that drew a man's attention. At least, they drew his attention. Not that *that* meant anything. It didn't. It meant less than nothing, yet somehow, he couldn't seem to tear his gaze away from her.

She was utterly absorbed in her book, her face alight, her lower lip caught between her teeth, and her legs swinging, the heels of her shoes hitting the side of the chair with a rhythmic thump. The morning sun streamed through the doors behind her, picking out the golden threads in her dark hair.

How had he ever let her fool him into thinking she was only passably pretty? She was a fascinating study in contrasts, with those sweet, soft pink lips hiding that barbed tongue and those mild blue eyes that sparked fire when her temper was roused. Looking at her now, it seemed incredible he could have ever thought her ordinary.

There was nothing ordinary about Euphemia Templeton.

He could have stayed there all afternoon watching her, but they didn't have much time. His aunt and Harriett would wake in a few hours. Until then, he and Miss Templeton had some business to attend to.

Private business.

He slipped out from behind the door, but she was so captivated by her book she didn't look up. He drew closer, but the thick carpeting muffled the sound of his boots, and still, she didn't notice him.

My, that must be a fascinating book, indeed. "What are you reading, Miss Templeton?"

"Oh!" She jerked upright at the sound of his voice. The book slipped from her hands, and fell to the floor with a thump. "Lord Fairmont! Dear God, where did you come from? Were you..." She glanced at the door, then back at him, her mouth falling open. "Were you *hiding* behind the door?"

"I wouldn't say hiding, no. I do beg your pardon. I didn't mean to startle you."

She glared at him. "If you didn't mean to startle me, then why were you lurking behind the door in the last place in the world anyone would expect to find you, and where you couldn't be seen?"

"I told you once already, Miss Templeton. Gentlemen don't lurk."

"No, you said gentlemen don't *skulk*, but alas, Lord Fairmont, for a gentleman who claims to do neither, you spend a lot of time leaping out from behind closed doors."

He strode across the room, took up the book she'd dropped, and turned it over in his hand. "The Devil's Elixirs." He glanced at her, manfully suppressing his smile. "Good God, Miss Templeton. I had no idea you had such... titillating taste in literature. I'm shocked to find my aunt even owns such a book."

Her eyes narrowed. "Are you laughing at me, Lord Fairmont?"

"No, indeed. I wouldn't dare." He leafed through the pages, his eyebrows aloft. "'*The choirmaster had a sister, who, without being an absolute beauty, was yet in the highest bloom of youth, and especially on account of her figure, was what is called a very charming girl.*' The choirmaster's sister, Miss Templeton? How scandalous."

"If I might have my book back, my lord?" She held out her hand.

He handed her the book and dropped into the chair across from hers. They sat there for a moment, staring at each other, neither of them speaking a word, until at last she cleared her throat. "It's rather early in the morning for a call, my lord."

"I rise before seven every morning, so I might take a ride before breakfast. I realize it's disgracefully unfashionable of me to be so industrious. I daresay the *ton* would be shocked, but I've never taken any pleasure in lazing about in my bed. There's no honor in wasting time, Miss Templeton."

"No, I suppose there isn't." She stole a look at him from under her thick eyelashes. He wasn't wearing riding clothes, and she frowned as she took him in. "Have you already had your ride this morning?"

"I have not. I chose to forgo my ride, as I have other, more pressing business to attend to this morning."

"I see." She cleared her throat again, fiddling with the edges of the book.

She *didn't* see— not yet —but she would. He leaned toward her, his gaze catching hers before she could look away. "My business, Miss Templeton, is with *you*."

"*Me*? What sort of business can you possibly have with me? Unless... is this about our, er, discussion last night?"

"In a manner of speaking, yes."

"I didn't intend to... it was wrong of me to speak to you so frankly, my lord. I'd rather hoped we might forget the entire conversation."

"Forget it? Oh no, Miss Templeton. I'm afraid it's too late for that."

Her blue eyes went wide, and a faint tinge of pink washed her cheeks. "I own I was... it wasn't at all polite of me to... if this is about..." She struggled upright, wincing as the book slid from her lap once again, and dropped to the floor. "It was kind of you to ask me to dance, Lord Fairmont, and very wrong of me to... to—"

"Run away from me?"

She huffed out a breath. "Yes. That. It was dreadfully rude of me, and I beg your pardon."

"I don't care about the dance, Miss Templeton. I didn't come here this morning to demand your apologies." He could simply tell her what he wanted— it would be the gentlemanly thing to do —but he rather liked keeping her off balance.

If ever there was a lady who'd benefit from a surprise or two, it was Euphemia Templeton.

So, he sat back, watching lazily as her blush intensified into a warm surge of scarlet burning in her cheeks, and seeping down the long, white column of her neck. She wasn't the first lady he'd ever made blush, but there was something delightful about *hers* and something ridiculously satisfying about being the cause of it.

But finally, he took pity on her. "Not but that's a very pretty apology, Miss Templeton. Still, I didn't come in search of you to scold you for last night."

"No?" Her brows drew together. "Why did you come, then?"

She wasn't going to like this. It would be a devil of a job to persuade her to go along with it, but alas for

Miss Templeton, he could be just as stubborn as she was.

This time, she wasn't going to have her way.

"Lord Fairmont? Did you hear me? I asked why you've come."

"I did hear you, yes." He plucked up the book from the floor and held it out to her, his gaze holding hers. "I've come, Miss Templeton, to teach you to waltz."

TWELVE

S he must have misheard him, because it
sounded as if he'd just said he'd come here to
teach her to waltz, and that... well, that was
impossible.

How would she ever have come up with such an
idea? He didn't know she'd never learned to waltz.

Unless... had Harriett told him? Or had he come to
his own conclusions from her absurd flight through
the ballroom last night? Oh, when would she learn to
stop overreacting, and giving herself away?

She eyed him, searching for any hint of what was
going on inside that handsome head of his, but he
merely gazed silently back at her. She couldn't read
his expression, but he was gazing at her so intently, it
was as if he weren't looking *at* her, but *into* her, and
prying loose every one of her secrets from their hiding
places.

As if he could *see* her.

She clutched at the book in her hand, squeezing
until her fingertips turned white. "It's kind of you to
offer, my lord, but I don't require waltzing lessons."

There, that would do. She hadn't claimed to know

how to waltz, so she hadn't lied, precisely, but neither had she—

"Yes, you do, Miss Templeton. Harriett told me you never learned to waltz."

Dash it. What did Harriett *mean*, spilling Phee's secrets to her brother?

"You've no need to be embarrassed." He leaned toward her, bracing his hands on his knees. "Harriett said you only had one season, and that it took place before waltzing was proper in London ballrooms. Thus, there's no reason you should have ever learned."

He knew about her failed season, as well? God above, was there anything Harriett *hadn't* told him? "I'm not embarrassed."

She was a trifle warm, that was all.

"Forgive me. It's just that your cheeks are a rather vivid red for a lady who isn't blushing, Miss Templeton." He raised an eyebrow, a suspicious twitching about his lips, and then...

Then, the man did something so awful, so dreadful, for an instant she could only gape at him in horrified shock.

He smiled.

The blasted man *smiled*. It started with that telltale quirk at the corners of his lips, and then the rest of his mouth curved upward into an honest-to-goodness grin.

Why, how *dare* he smile so charmingly at her?

How dare he have such a charming smile at all? How dare it take over his whole face, changing his demeanor entirely? Such a man should have a tight smile, a stiff, half-curve of his lips, not this lovely, boyish one that lit him up and made his eyes twinkle.

Wasn't he handsome enough, without that smile? It wasn't *fair*, dash it—

"Miss Templeton? Are you unwell? Your eyes have gone a bit glassy."

"I, ah..." Say something, for pity's sake! "Very well, Lord Fairmont. I don't deny that I don't know how to waltz. Harriett is quite right in saying I never learned. What I meant is, I don't need you to teach me, because I will never have occasion to waltz."

"Of course, you'll have occasion to waltz. Lady Upton's ball is the week after next."

"I'm aware of that, my lord, but I don't intend to dance at Lady Upton's ball." She hadn't danced at a ball since her first season, and she wasn't going to start with Lady Upton's. Indeed, if she could manage it without offending Harriett and Lady Fosberry, she wouldn't attend Lady Upton's ball at all.

He leaned back in his chair, that shrewd gaze still pinning her down, missing nothing—not the merest twitch, or catch of her breath. "I had a word with Harriett last night, when we arrived home after Lord Powell's ball," he said at last. "I told her I'd noticed you go to some lengths to avoid drawing attention to yourself, and she agreed that was true."

For pity's sake! She loved Harriett dearly, and yet at that moment, she would happily have delivered her a blistering scold that would have left her ears ringing for days.

"Why don't you ever dance, Miss Templeton?"

She started to reply, but before she could say a word, he held up his hand. "A warning first. If you're about to tell me you're too old to dance, then you may as well preserve your breath. It's utter nonsense, and I think you know that."

"That wasn't what I was going to say." It was a lie, of course. She'd been about to tell him it didn't become spinsters to dance, but if she said it now, he'd only argue with her, and it would prolong what was becoming a rather awkward conversation.

What was she to say, then? She couldn't invent something— not with those clever blue eyes on her, assessing her every move.

That left nothing but the truth. Or a partial truth, at any rate. "I suppose Harriett is right, my lord. I don't care for people staring at me."

And they would, if she took to the dance floor at Lady Upton's ball. They'd stare and smirk themselves into a frenzy, and it would be worse than it had been at Lord Powell's ball last night.

Lord Fairmont wouldn't understand it, of course. He'd laugh at her now, or scoff at her for being such a coward, and perhaps it was nothing less than she deserved, but somehow, she couldn't bear to look into his eyes when he did it.

She dropped her gaze to the book in her lap and waited.

But the mockery never came.

"I'm not surprised at it, Miss Templeton. My aunt tells me the *ton* has been unkind to the Templetons since your family's scandal, but I confess I didn't realize how bad it was until last night."

She jerked her head up, her breath catching hard in her throat.

She'd heard Lord Fairmont speak condescendingly, and she'd heard him speak mockingly. She'd heard his voice heavy with arrogance, sarcasm, or irritability. She'd heard him bark orders in a tone that sent the servants scurrying.

But never, not once, had she ever heard him speak *gently* before. Yet there was no other way to describe that soft inflection in his voice, that hint of compassion.

It was... dear God, he could coax the very birds from the trees with that voice.

"But it's been six years since then, Euphemia," he went on. "Six years is a long time to hide." He hesitated but then reached out, and laid his hand over hers. "Allow me to teach you to waltz. Dance with me at Lady Upton's ball, and show the *ton* you're no longer afraid of them."

She wanted to. Oh, yes, there was a part of her that wanted to show them she didn't care a fig for their sneers and smirks, to show them that they couldn't cow her, but the truth was, she *was* afraid of them. Six years was a long time, just as he'd said.

So long, she could no longer remember how to be brave.

Slowly, she drew her hand out from under his. "You're very kind, Lord Fairmont, but I-I can't."

She stilled, waiting for his reply, but he said nothing for some time.

Then he rose without a word and made his way to the door.

But just as she was drawing a relieved breath, he stopped on the threshold.

"I'll return tomorrow, and ask you again, and then again, the day after that. I'll keep coming, Euphemia, and I'll keep asking until you give me the answer I want."

And then he was gone, closing the door quietly behind him.

~

PHEE SPENT the rest of the day fretting about... well, everything.

Arrogant earls, Lady Upton, the *ton*, the waltz. She was so distracted that even *The Devil's Elixir* couldn't hold her attention.

It was an excessively long day, but by the time she retired to her bedchamber that evening, she'd mostly convinced herself that Lord Fairmont would grow bored with his game, and give up this nonsense about teaching her to waltz.

But alas, Lord Fairmont turned out to be as good as his word.

He appeared the following morning, and then again the morning after that. On the third day, she'd taken a breakfast tray in her room in order to avoid him, but when she'd emerged, she'd found him lounging against the wall across from her bedchamber, a smirk on his lips.

Every day, he asked again if he might teach her to waltz, and every day, she refused him.

On the sixth morning after Lord Powell's ball, she woke very early and sneaked off to Lady Fosberry's private parlor for her breakfast, but before she'd managed to take a single sip of tea, he appeared in the doorway, that same maddening grin twitching at his lips.

"Ah, here you are, Miss Templeton." He dropped onto a settee, crossed one long leg over the other knee, and turned that penetrating blue gaze on her. "If I didn't know it to be impossible, I might suspect you of hiding from me."

"It hasn't done me any good so far, has it?" No

matter what corner she attempted to duck into, or what hallways she scurried down, he always seemed to find her.

He was nothing, if not utterly determined.

It didn't make any *sense*, dash it.

She'd lain wide awake in her bed every night since this nonsense about the waltz began, puzzling over it. Why was he so insistent upon teaching her to waltz? Why should he care if she danced, or not? She'd be gone from London soon enough, and goodness knew once she was out of his sight, he'd never spare her another thought.

Try as she might, she couldn't think of a single thing a fashionable gentleman like Lord Fairmont had to gain from teaching a disgraced spinster like her how to waltz.

But this morning, something had changed.

She'd woken in the early hours, before sunrise, the last rays of pale moonlight peeking through a gap in the draperies, bathing her bed in a silvery glow.

Her body was relaxed, still drowsy with the last vestiges of sleep, and her mind was calm.

For the first time since he'd proposed his absurd waltzing idea, she wasn't thinking about Lord Fairmont.

That is, not entirely. He was still in her thoughts, as he always seemed to be these days, that boyish grin haunting her dreams, but for once, he'd retreated to the murky shadows at the back of her mind.

But this time, for the first time in the past six nights, when she woke, she was thinking about herself.

No, not six nights. Six *years*.

It had been six years since her mother had dis-

ANNA BRADLEY

graced their family by absconding to the Continent with her married lover, leaving Phee's heartbroken father and her four younger sisters behind.

Between her sisters' needs and the sharp decline in her father's health, there'd been no time for anything but doing what must be done to see the family through it. Tilly had only been thirteen then, and Helena just fourteen. Juliet and Emmeline had done all they could to help her, but as the eldest, she'd taken most of the responsibility on her own shoulders.

She'd never regretted it. That was what one did, for the family they loved.

But in all those years, she'd rarely spared a thought for herself.

Not because she was selfless, or self-sacrificing—it was nothing so noble as that —but because there hadn't been *time*.

There'd been no time to think, or dream, or fall in love. No time for balls, or pretty dresses, or midnight blue ribbons in her hair.

No time to dance.

She'd loved dancing, once. Oh, she'd never been particularly good at it. She'd always been a trifle awkward, despite the endless dance lessons her mother had forced her to endure, and goodness knew, there was no dance more intimidating than a waltz.

Juliet once told her that a waltz was like a minuet, but it didn't look like any minuet she'd ever danced. All that twirling about! How did one keep from becoming dizzy, and toppling over?

She could find out for herself if she wished to. If she was brave enough.

And maybe— just maybe —she *was* brave enough.

154

At least, a part of her was, because when she woke this morning, she didn't ask herself why Lord Fairmont insisted on teaching her to waltz.

Instead, she asked herself what possible reason she had to refuse him.

The only answer she could come up with was cowardice.

Pure cowardice. Somehow, in the last six years, she'd become a coward.

It wasn't a particularly flattering discovery. Understandable, yes, given the scorn the *ton* had heaped upon the Templetons after her mother's disgrace, but how long was she going to keep hiding from the *ton*?

It had been six years already.

She could spend another six years darting around corners and hiding in alcoves. Another six years of shrinking back from the stares, and cowering from the whispers and smirks. Another six years of being unable to face her own reflection in the looking glass.

Or she could accept Lord Fairmont's invitation, and learn to dance a waltz.

It was only a waltz. Just a waltz.

"No, Miss Templeton, hiding *won't* do you any good. No good at all."

She jerked her attention back to Lord Fairmont.

"How do you get on with *The Devil's Elixir*?" He nodded at the book resting in her lap. "Has the good friar drunk the poisonous brew yet?"

She glanced down at the sketch opposite the title page of the book she'd found this morning, tucked among the other dancing manuals on a high shelf in Lady Fosberry's library. It was a pretty sketch of a ballroom with elaborately dressed windows in the background, and in the foreground...

Dancers. Eighteen of them, the gentlemen dressed in smart, double-breasted tailcoats, and each of them partnering a lady in a ballgown with elaborate ruffles at the hem. Nine couples on the verge of embarking upon a waltz.

She'd brought the book into the parlor because she'd meant to have a private look at it before she accepted Lord Fairmont's offer, but he'd found her out, and really, what was the sense in putting it off?

Either she was going to learn to waltz, or she wasn't.

She took a deep breath, her heart pounding. "It's, ah... it's not *The Devil's Elixir*."

"No?" He raised an eyebrow. "What is it?"

Once she told him, there would be no going back, but perhaps... well, perhaps she'd spent enough time going backward to last her a lifetime.

She looked up from the book and met his gaze. "It's Thomas Wilson's *A Description of the Correct Method of Waltzing*."

He hadn't expected *that*. For an instant, he only stared at her, his blue eyes wide, but then a slow smile curved his lips. "Is that so?"

How satisfying it was, to surprise a man like Lord Fairmont. How utterly delicious, to be the one who put such a smile on his face. Perhaps she should be worried at just how satisfying it was, how delicious.

Or perhaps she should cease worrying for once, and do as she pleased. "I do hope you don't regret your offer to teach me, my lord. Alas, I'm not one of those ladies with a natural affinity for dancing. It's quite a task you've undertaken."

"You don't frighten me, Miss Templeton. A challenging task is always more satisfying than a simple one." His smile widened. "Don't you agree?"

That smile... dear God, there was no not answering it with one of her own, was there? "We'll see if you still think so after a day or two of dragging me about the dance floor. I daresay it will be rather like lugging a dead body through the figures."

If she'd ever been any good at twirling about a dance floor, the idea of standing up in a ballroom with Lord Fairmont while all the *ton* stared at them wouldn't have terrified her as it did.

"All these instructions." She tapped the page in front of her. "It looks dreadfully complicated. So many circles."

"The waltz is essentially a circle of couples moving within another, larger circle."

"What's this?" She turned the book toward him, so he might see the sketch.

"See the numbers here?" He pointed to the number one printed underneath the sketch of the first couple. "There are nine different positions—"

"*Nine*? Oh, dear God."

He laughed. "There's no reason for you to look so alarmed, Miss Templeton. It's a dance, not a beheading." He rose to his feet as he spoke, and held out his hand to her. "Shall we, then?"

"Where are we going?" She eyed his outstretched hand, nerves fluttering in her belly.

"The ballroom, of course. You can't learn to waltz in here, with all these settees and tables about. There's much more room in the ballroom, and no one will disturb us there."

"Are you quite certain, my lord, that you wish to go through with this?"

2

Did she hope he'd say no— that he'd changed his mind, and no longer wished to embark on this mad scheme? It would be easier that way, and yet...

She *didn't* wish it. Now she'd made up her mind to take the first step, she couldn't take it fast enough.

She swallowed, waiting for his answer.

"I am quite certain. If the French and the Germans can manage the waltz, then you can, as well." He reached for her hand then, caught it in his, and tugged her to her feet.

His long, elegant fingers curled around hers, warm and strong, his fine kid gloves as smooth as cream under her fingertips.

And for a moment, just one, breathless moment...

She might have followed him anywhere.

CHAPTER
THIRTEEN

E uphemia Templeton did *not* know how to
dance a waltz.

James had half-suspected she was exag-
gerating her ignorance— he'd never met a lady more
likely to diminish her accomplishments than Euphemia was —but this time, she'd been telling the
truth.

When the dance called for the left foot, she invari-
ably began on her right. She slid when she was meant
to step, confused the direction when she turned, and
shifted sideways when she was meant to come
forward.

She was perfectly awful, yet it was the most delightful waltz he'd ever danced.

It wasn't at all charitable of him to find her confusion so charming, to revel in her stuttered apologies,
but her blushes were so adorable that his lips insisted
upon grinning, despite his every attempt to maintain
a dignified expression.

"Let's start again, shall we? Place your hand on
my *right* shoulder, and... er, no, you'll begin on your

left foot, so it should be in front... yes, like that. Now, rest your fingertips in my left hand, and—"

"Lord Fairmont?"

"Yes, Miss Templeton?"

"I beg your pardon, but you're *quite* sure your right arm is meant to be behind my back, with your hand, er... just *there*, are you not?"

It was the third time she'd asked, and every time his palm found the soft place between her shoulder blades, a tiny tremor passed through her. It was either extremely flattering or extremely humbling.

He wasn't certain which.

"I am indeed, Miss Templeton. I assure you, this is the proper pose for the second position, but if it's unacceptable to you, then perhaps we could—"

"No, no. It's perfectly acceptable. I beg your pardon, my lord. Do go on."

"Very good. Now, as we move into the third position, you'll turn to face me, and... no, the other direction, Miss Templeton."

She bit her lip, her cheeks coloring. "I did warn you I'd be hopeless at this, my lord."

"You're far from hopeless, Euph— er, Miss Templeton. You're simply learning, that's all. Now, we'll be facing each other in third position, like this." He turned her to his left, so her back was to the window. "You see, I still have your hand in mine?"

"I— yes."

Was she a trifle breathless?

"Is your right foot forward?" His voice was a bit husky, and he was obliged to clear his throat. "Yes, very good. As we move into fourth position, you'll raise your right arm over your head and clasp my left hand, then we'll execute a half turn to the right, and

— no, *my* right, Miss Templeton. Careful, or you'll—"

But his warning came too late. She turned to her right just as he lifted his arm, and somehow, his elbow struck her temple. "Euphemia!"

"Ouch."

It wasn't a sharp blow— thankfully, his coat provided some padding —but it caught her off guard, knocking her back a step.

She stumbled, her feet tangling underneath her. "Oh, dear. I do beg your pardon, my lord."

He caught her upper arms and pulled her into him, steadying her against his chest. "Good God, are you alright?"

"I-I think so." She was rubbing a spot near her right eye. "Although I do feel a bit as if I crashed into a tree."

"I'm sorry. I wasn't paying proper attention."

"Not at all, Lord Fairmont. It was my error. I turned the wrong way. Again." She looked up at him, a sheepish grin on her lips. "The waltz is more dangerous than I imagined."

"I, ah, think it's generally considered safe enough." Why was he still holding her against his chest? She was perfectly steady now.

"Are you implying, Lord Fairmont, that I'm the only lady in England clumsy enough to concuss herself during a waltz?"

"Certainly not. I'd never imply such a thing. I'd say it aloud." He gazed down at her, grinning like a fool, when the proper thing to do would be to release her, at once.

Release her, for God's sake.

But that wasn't what he did. Instead, he gazed

down into her startled blue eyes, an odd hitch in his breath.

She was wearing another one of her seemingly endless supply of somber gowns this morning— this one a dull, dark green, but somehow, he still couldn't tear his gaze away from her. With her flushed cheeks, and the wisps of hair that had escaped her severe bun curling around her face, she was more beautiful to him than ever.

There was no reason she should be. No reason at all that those wispy curls should fascinate him, but all at once his skin felt too tight for his body, and his lower belly bottomed out in the way it did right before...

Oh, no. His cock was choosing *now* to make its presence known? It was the rudest organ imaginable.

He released her and took a step back, but she was still rubbing her temple, and without thinking, he brushed her hand aside with gentle fingertips. Surely, he wasn't such a savage he couldn't control himself for long enough to make certain she wasn't hurt?

"Does it hurt still? Here, come closer to the window, into the light."

"It's a little tender." She let out a nervous laugh as he led her toward the window. "You have hard elbows, Lord Fairmont."

And an even harder cock, but God it was making enough of a nuisance of itself without his dwelling on it.

"Let me see." He swept the wispy curls aside and leaned closer. Her temple looked a little red, but it wasn't swelling, so—

Wait, were those little gold flecks in her eyes? Or was he imagining them?

He wasn't. There was a ring of gold flecks surrounding her pupils in a most enchanting starburst pattern, like dappled sunlight on dark blue water.

"Is it very bad, my lord?"

He sucked in a quick breath to steady himself, but she was so close, her sweet pink mouth just a breath away from his. "No, but it looks a little red. Are you dizzy at all?"

"I-I don't think so, no." Her whisper was shaky, her blue eyes wide, but she didn't move away.

He had no reason to keep touching her— no right to touch her at all —but his hands were sliding up her arms to her shoulders, his palms cupping the soft, warm skin of her neck. "Euphemia."

"Yes?" She swallowed.

He swept his fingers over her throat to feel the movement, then brushed his lips over the red mark on her temple. "Does this hurt?"

She drew in an unsteady breath. "No."

He traced her jaw, then tipped her face up to his with a finger under her chin. He waited for one breath, two, to give her a chance to pull away, but she only gazed up at him, her blue eyes soft, and her lips parted.

Just like that, he was lost.

His aunt, his sister, Lady Upton's ball, the waltz... it all faded away. Time narrowed and contracted until there was just the two of them, her face tipped up to his, their breath mingling.

"And this?" He pressed his lips to her forehead again, lingering this time, his lips parted now, and his heart pounding at the sensation of her smooth skin against his tongue. "Does this hurt?"

She moved her hands to his chest and he stiffened. If she pushed him away, he'd release her at once. He wouldn't frighten her for the world.

But she only rested her hands against him, her palms flat against his waistcoat. "No. Your, ah... your lips are soft. Much softer than I imagined."

"You imagined my lips?" Good God, he wanted to sink to his knees for her.

"No! I mean, I..." She pulled back a little, her cheeks burning.

But now that he knew how it felt to have her in his arms, he could no longer ignore the truth. It crashed into him, the impact so sudden, there was no denying it.

He wanted her there, in his arms. They'd been so empty without her.

He couldn't let her go without one kiss. Just one, a brush of his lips against hers.

Surely, he could control himself long enough for one innocent kiss?

He stroked his thumb down her cheek and teased it across her lower lip, testing the plumpness of that tender pink skin.

Once, and then again, and then as naturally as taking a breath, his lips were on hers.

He coaxed her gently until she opened her mouth with a soft moan. He kissed her deeply then, sinking his hands into her hair, the long strands catching on his fingers as he urged her mouth against his.

When he raised his head to look into her face she was gazing back at him, her eyes a dark, endless blue, and her mouth the sweetest thing he'd ever tasted, like tea, and a hint of sugar, and *her*.

She traced a shy finger around his lips, following

the upward curve of his mouth as he smiled down at her.

She smiled back. "Softer, and warmer, too."

"Phee." Nothing could have stopped him from taking her mouth again then, a little more insistently this time, the tip of his tongue sweeping over the seam of her lips.

She opened for him without any hesitation, her fingers curling into his waistcoat.

He slipped his tongue inside, a low groan vibrating in his chest as their tongues tangled together, each slick caress driving him wild until he tore his mouth away at last before he could no longer resist taking more than a kiss.

Yet he couldn't let her go, either.

He let his mouth graze her ear, just the lightest caress of his lips as he whispered, "Do you ever think about me, Euphemia? Did you think of me that day we walked together in the garden? Or when we played chess together? Did you retire to your bedchamber that night, and think about me?"

He nuzzled her neck, unable to help himself.

She dropped her head back to give him better access, trembling against him. "I... yes, but... not only then."

He groaned at her words. Dear God, but this was dangerous. Anyone could walk into the ballroom at any time, and with each of her sighs, each fevered breath between them, his control was slipping.

Just one more kiss...

He opened his mouth against her neck and let his tongue dart out to taste her.

She made a sound then, something between a sigh and a gasp.

He trailed his lips over her neck, suckling at her, then soothing her with gentle strokes of his tongue. "Have you ever thought of me when you're alone in your room, in your bed?"

She grasped a handful of his shirt in her fist to steady herself as she rose to her toes to get her neck closer to his seeking lips. "Yes."

He let out a desperate moan. Had she thought about him and touched herself? His cock went hard as steel for her at the thought, but as much as he wanted to hear her tell him she *had*— she *did* —he couldn't ask her. She was an innocent, and he—

He was meant to be a gentleman, but he'd never felt less like one than he did now.

A gentleman didn't devour an innocent lady in his aunt's ballroom.

She slid her hands up his chest and wrapped her arms around his neck so her breasts were pressed against him, and brought her lips to his throat, catching a tiny fold of his skin between her teeth and nipping at him.

He shuddered against her. God help him, but she didn't kiss like an innocent.

She kissed like a woman who knew what she wanted, and he thought he'd go crazy from the sensation of her warm breath drifting over the damp patch she'd made on his throat.

He had to let her go. *Now.*

But he was losing this battle, losing himself to her with every heated breath that passed between them, and instead of letting her go as a proper gentleman should, he eased her backward until she was against the wall behind them, his body pressed closely against hers so he could feel the shape of her thighs and her breasts and dear God, she felt so good, so perfect, her slender curves softening his hard angles, her belly cradling his erection.

She moaned, and he whispered to her, his mouth hot against her ear. "I've thought of you, too. Of touching you here."

He teased his finger over the modest scooped neckline of her dress, lingering at the place where the dark green linen gave way to her silky skin. "I could spend hours here, kissing your skin, tracing it with my tongue."

She sagged against him as if her knees had buckled, and he slid his hand down to her waist, holding her more firmly against him. "Do you taste sweet here, Euphemia?"

She let out a choked whimper. "I-I don't know."

"Shall I tell you?" He bent over her, dropping a tender kiss over the hollow of her throat.

"Yes." She caught a handful of his hair, and dragged his head down, toward the tempting shadows between her breasts. "Please."

He was so close, so close to tasting that silky skin—

"...mistress has asked that we see to it the stained glass window at the end of the hallway is cleaned, Becky."

Euphemia tensed against him. "James."

He froze. Two sets of footsteps were coming down the hallway.

"You may as well begin on the windows in the ballroom. We're sure to have a ball in there before season's end. I'll send Sarah upstairs to help you."

"Yes, Mr. Watkins."

There was a pause, then a moment later one of

the housemaids passed the ballroom and continued toward the far end of the hallway. Thankfully, she didn't glance inside, and Watkins must have gone to fetch the other housemaid because he didn't appear.

James looked down at Euphemia, still clasped in his arms. Her eyes were wide, and the fetching pink color had drained from her cheeks.

What was he *doing*? They were standing in his aunt's house, where anyone could come across them at any time, and he'd been about to... what? Lower her bodice? Undress her? Then what? Would he have hiked her skirts up, and taken her on the ballroom floor?

He eased her out of his arms, but he dropped a kiss on her forehead before he made himself let her go. He had to kiss her again, but he didn't dare take her lips, or God only knew what would happen.

"Euphemia." He eased her gently away from him and stepped back, putting a safe distance between them. "I should never have... this went much too far, and I beg your pardon most sincerely."

She looked dazed, her blue eyes hazy, but she shook her head. "It wasn't only you, James. Although I did try to warn you the waltz was dangerous, did I not?"

He stared at her. Could he have heard her correctly? Had she just made a *joke*?

She gave him a hesitant smile. "I begin to understand why Almack's forbid it for all those years."

As soon as he saw her smile, all the tension eased out of him. He should be ashamed of himself, and he *was*, yet there was that same helpless grin from earlier, curving his lips.

"I'd quite like to learn it still, however," she went

on, casting him a shy glance. "If you're still willing to teach it to me, that is."

"Of course, I am." He held out his hand because he needed to touch her just one more time. She took it, and he squeezed before letting her go. "It would be my honor, Miss Templeton."

FOURTEEN

T hey were going to be late for Lady Upton's ball.

James threw himself into a chair in the corner of his dressing room and waved an impatient hand at Lord Gilbert. "Remove that cravat at once, Gilbert. It's a disgrace. Crosby, if you'd be so good as to assist Lord Gilbert?"

"Yes, my lord."

Crosby hurried across the dressing room toward Gilly, who was studying his reflection in the looking glass with a bemused expression. "What's wrong with my cravat?"

"It's limp, Gilbert. *Limp*. It hasn't been properly starched, and the silk is of inferior quality. A gentleman's linen must always be flawless, and *that*." James pointed at the wilted scrap of cloth around Gilbert's neck. "Is *far* from flawless."

All of his careful planning, foiled by a limp cravat.

He'd hoped to arrive at Lady Upton's ball before Euphemia did, so he might scowl any of the *ton* who dared to laugh at her into silence, but he couldn't allow Gilbert to walk into Lady Upton's ballroom looking like he'd been dragged through a knothole. Thank God he'd had the foresight to insist Gilbert collect him at his lodgings in St. James on his way to the ball this evening.

He'd suspected something like this would happen.

Gilbert had made great strides forward since he'd appeared in the Ring in that monstrous canary-yellow coat, but one did like to keep a close eye on one's charge, and Gilbert did still occasionally make the sort of faux pas that would earn him the scorn of other gentlemen.

He couldn't allow that. Gilbert was going to marry Harriett, and thus, he must be above all reproach.

Gilbert hadn't ventured to ask for Harriett's hand yet, but he would, and it would be soon. He'd almost done so during their ride yesterday. James had done his best to appear unthreatening, but after much stuttering and blushing, Gilbert's courage had failed him.

At this rate, Gilbert might never work up the nerve to ask his permission to court Harriett, and they'd never have this business over with. Not that he'd made it easy for the boy. To be fair, he'd been rather a bear about it all, especially at the beginning.

But Harriett had been right about Gilbert. He was a decent fellow— even rather clever on occasion, shockingly enough, and he adored Harriett, which was all that mattered.

Perhaps a tiny nudge in the right direction was in order.

James rose to his feet, plucking up Gilly's coat from the chair before joining Gilly at the looking glass. "Weston?" he asked, fingering the black superfine.

Gilly gave an eager nod. "Yes, indeed, Lord Fairmont, just as you recommended."

"Good man." He slapped Gilly on the shoulder. "Fetch one of my silk cravats for Lord Gilbert, Crosby."

"Yes, my lord." Crosby crossed to the chest of drawers and withdrew one of the dozen lengths of flawless silk from the drawer.

"A Gordian Knot, I think, Crosby. What say you?"

"An ideal choice, my lord." Crosby draped the silk around Gilly's neck, fussing with the folds until he'd created the perfect Gordian Knot. "There we are. Very nice indeed, Lord Gilbert."

James cocked his head. "It's not quite right yet. Something's missing."

"What?" Gilly frowned at his reflection in the glass. "Do I need more hair pomade?"

"No, that's not it." James went to the rosewood jewel chest in the corner of his dressing room and rummaged through the velvet trays until he found a gold cravat pin set with a tiny emerald. "This belonged to my grandfather." He unclasped the pin, fitted it among the snowy folds of Gilbert's cravat, and then stepped back to admire the effect. "Yes, that will do."

Gilly reached up to finger the pin, his hand shaking. "That's kind of you, Lord Fairmont."

"It suits you, Gilbert. I've got another one very much like it, so you may as well keep this one."

"Keep it? That's..." Gilly stared at his reflection in the glass, his eyes bright. "I don't know what to say, my lord."

"There's no need to say anything at all," James said gruffly, clearing his throat. "No theatrics, Gilbert, I beg you."

Gilly swallowed. "I…"

Ah, here it was. Three, two, one—

"I want to marry Lady Harriett!" Gilbert blurted, then flushed up to the roots of his hair.

James hid his smile. "I rather suspected you did."

"May I have your permission to… that is, her hand, Lord Fairmont. May I have the honor of…" Gilly blew out a breath, then gathered himself together, straightened his shoulders, and turned to meet James's eyes. "I love her very much, my lord, and I promise you I'll devote myself to making her happy."

"Well, Gilbert, I can't ask for more than that, can I?"

Gilbert gaped at him, eyes wide, as if he couldn't quite believe it could be as easy as that. "Er, no?"

"No. You're a good man, Gilbert." He laid a hand on Gilbert's shoulder. "I think you'll make Harriett a fine husband."

"Thank you, my lord." Gilbert reached into his coat pocket, withdrew a handkerchief, and mopped his brow with it. "I feel a bit faint."

"No time for a swoon now, Gilbert. Come, let's get on with it, shall we? I wish to dance a waltz with Euphemia Templeton tonight."

~

PHEE HOVERED in the doorway of Lady Upton's ballroom, taking in the bright silks and satins, the flashing jewels, and the dozens upon dozens of flushed faces.

Familiar faces. Here were all the same fashionable aristocrats who attended every ball, all of them laughing and gossiping about the same things they'd laughed and gossiped about the week before.

She might have been standing at the doors to Lord Powell's ballroom, or any other ballroom, at any week throughout the season.

It was a crush, of course, and dreadfully hot, the humidity from too many bodies pressed too closely together assaulting her even from this distance, causing a trickle of perspiration to slide down her spine.

She might have been hovering at the entrance to hell itself.

Goodness knew she'd rather take her chances with demons armed with pitchforks than face the *ton* tonight. Her heart was thrashing so wildly against her ribs that for one awful moment her head went all wobbly on her neck, her lung squeezing helplessly, desperate for air. If she didn't manage a deep breath, she'd fall into a swoon, and that... no, that wouldn't do.

Not tonight.

Tonight's ball *wasn't* the same, because this time, she wouldn't be running away.

"You don't have a thing to worry about, Phee." Harriett laid a comforting hand on Phee's shoulder. "They don't matter. They never have."

"No, indeed," Lady Fosberry echoed. "They're all shameful, wicked creatures, to be sure, but no matter what they do or say, just remember, dearest, that you have as much right to be here as anyone else does."

Yes, she did. Oh, it might not feel like it *now*, as she took in the faces closest to her. All the people who'd laughed at her last time were here again tonight— Lady Ellsworth, Lady Silvester, and Lady Arundel —and her heart gave its usual spasm of dread.

But they couldn't hurt her. Not unless she permitted them to do so, and that, she would not do.

Not this time.

"We're sure about this gown, then?" She smoothed her hands down her shimmering silk skirts. Inside her gloves, her palms were damp.

Harriett smiled. "I've never been more sure of anything in my life."

"It's perfection, Euphemia. Utter perfection, and you, my dear, are perfection in it." Lady Fosberry gave a decisive nod. "Now, shall we bid Lady Upton a good evening?"

"Yes, I'm ready." This was it, then. There was no turning back now.

She drew in a deep, calming breath, lifted her chin, and stepped into the ballroom.

Almost immediately, there was a gasp, high-pitched, and breathy.

It was Lady Ellsworth, of course. Her ladyship had perfected her scandalized gasps. Phee would have known it anywhere, so many times had she heard it.

Her ladyship stared at her as she passed, her outraged gaze sweeping over Phee's gown, a gloved hand over her gaping mouth.

Oh, dear. It appeared as if Lady Ellsworth did not approve of the frock she'd chosen to wear this evening. Perhaps it was the color. It *was* a bold shade of blue and despite the modest neckline, rather revealing, the bodice clinging to her as if it were a second skin. The back was cut rather lower than was strictly appropriate, as well, revealing a generous expanse of the bare skin of her neck, shoulders, and back.

Scandalous, particularly for a spinster.

But if a lady had made up her mind to challenge the *ton* by dancing the waltz with a gentleman as fashionable as Lord Fairmont, there was no sense in doing the thing halfway, was there?

No, an occasion such as this called for a particular sort of gown, a gown that said she no longer cared about their whispers or their stares.

This was that gown.

It was blue, but not the pale, pastel blue favored by the younger ladies, or the celestial blue that was so fashionable this season. No, this was an entirely different blue, one rarely seen in a ballroom— a blue so vibrant, so vivid, the only proper word for it was azure.

Indeed, the gown was so eye-catching it verged on improper, and so it might have been, if it hadn't been made of delicate tissue silk so fine, so fragile, it floated like a dream around her as she made her way across the ballroom, the white sarsenet petticoat she wore underneath peeking out from beneath her hems as she walked, creating the effect of a cascading waterfall over a ripple of silvery foam.

Aside from a narrow band of French lace at the hem and a scattering of tiny pearl beads over the skirt, there were no trimmings.

The gown didn't need them.

Her only other ornament was a small diamond and sapphire pendant around her neck, and a white silk ribbon woven into the dark locks of her hair.

Heads turned as they made their way across the

ballroom toward Lady Upton, and whispers swelled in their wake, but this time, she didn't acknowledge them.

Harriett was right. They didn't matter.

Tonight, there was only one person who did matter.

Lord Fairmont.

James.

He wasn't in the ballroom. If he had been, she would have known it at once. She would have sensed him, just as one sensed the presence of someone beloved to them, beloved *by* them.

A dear friend, or a lover.

He hadn't kissed her since their first waltzing lesson. He'd appeared faithfully every morning, and with a gentle patience that she'd thought him incapable of only weeks earlier, he'd waltzed with her until she no longer had to think about the steps, but twirled about the empty ballroom in his arms as if she'd been made to dance with him.

As if they'd been made to dance together.

"Miss Templeton. How do you do?"

They'd reached the other end of the ballroom, and Phee dragged her attention to Lady Upton, who was regarding her with a kind smile on her face. "How wonderful it is, Miss Templeton, to see you looking so extremely well."

Phee smiled and pressed her ladyship's hand. "You're very kind, my lady."

"Indeed, Maria, you've always been a dear, sweet, creature." Lady Fosberry pressed an affectionate kiss to Lady Upton's cheek.

"Well, we do our best, do we not, Patience?" Lady Upton laughed as she took Harriett's hand. "Lady

Harriett! Goodness, how pretty you look! I daresay your dance card will be full this evening."

Harriett blushed. "Thank you, my lady."

"Now, Miss Templeton, may I introduce you to Lord Welles? He's just over there, and I do believe he's admiring you. It would give me great pleasure to see you dance this evening, and Lord Welles is a most delightful part—"

"That won't be necessary, Lady Upton."

Phee stilled. The voice came from behind her, the deep, rich timber of it sending goosebumps rushing to the surface of her skin. She turned, and there was Lord Fairmont, just as he'd promised he would be, so handsome in his black evening clothes a soft gasp dropped from her lips.

"Miss Templeton." His blue eyes gleamed as he took her in from head to toe in a thorough, heated perusal before he caught her hand, and raised it to his lips. "I pity the other ladies in the ballroom tonight."

"M-my lord?"

"None of them will ever dare wear blue again, after tonight."

There was nothing improper in his words, but his husky drawl, the sensual half smile on his lips, and the way his eyes darkened as they moved over her set her every nerve ending alight.

"My goodness," Lady Upton murmured, flapping her fan in front of her face.

"I believe the musicians are readying for a waltz." Lord Fairmont held out his hand to her. "May I have this dance, Miss Templeton?"

Six years of the *ton*'s scorn, six years of their smirks and whispers. Six years of loneliness, and shame, and heartbreak. Six years of hiding, of making herself as small as she could, and it had all come down to this moment.

Six years, one stubborn earl, a dozen waltzing lessons, and a single, devastating kiss.

Now here she was, her heart in her throat as she gazed up into the blue eyes of the only man who'd ever truly *seen* her.

She drew in deep breath, smiled up at him, and rested the tips of her fingers in the palm of his hand. "I will, indeed. Thank you, my lord."

It should have been terrifying, the moment his fingers closed around hers and he led her to the dance floor with the weight of dozens of curious gazes upon them.

If it had been anyone other than *him*, perhaps it would have been.

But the clasp of his fingers around hers, the warmth in his blue eyes, and that half-smile tugging at the corners of his lips were so familiar to her now, there was nothing strange in it, nothing to fear.

It felt like coming home.

"The left foot first," he whispered, grinning down at her as they took their places on the floor and assumed the first position. "You remember, don't you?"

"I do. I remember everything, my lord."

Every moment of every dance they'd shared in Lady Fosberry's empty ballroom was etched in her mind, a favorite image she'd come back to over and over again after she left London, and this strange interlude with him was nothing but a memory, a wonderful dream she'd once had, a long time ago.

But she was here now, and with every shared breath between them, she fell deeper into the moment, grasping at it with numb fingertips even as it slipped from her hands.

The firm, steady pressure of his fingers around hers, and the strength in his right shoulder under her fingertips. The dizzying slide of his hand across her back, and the thrill of his palm resting between her shoulder blades, left bare from the daring cut of her gown.

His touch burned her through the silk of his gloves, as if he held a flame in his hand, the heat setting her heart fluttering against her ribs. Her toes curled inside her silk slippers as they stood together, unmoving, waiting as the musicians finished turning their instruments.

They struck the first chord. It trembled there for an instant, high and sweet...

Then they were off, James sweeping her into the first turn, then the next, the world shifting and fragmenting into a blur of faces and colors and a swell of violin strings, the crushing weight of hundreds of eyes upon them.

She might have been frightened then if he hadn't pulled her closer, the long, lean muscles of his arm flexing against her waist, his voice a low rumble in her ear. "Look at me, Euphemia."

She lifted her gaze, her eyes finding his, so blue, sleepy under the weight of his thick lashes. He leaned closer, a lock of dark hair falling across his forehead, his breath stirring the wisps of hair at her temples. "You're safe."

And she was. Here, in his arms, she was safer than she'd ever been.

Safer, perhaps, than she'd ever be again.

The *ton* had already taken so much from her, but they couldn't have *this*.

She wouldn't let them.

So, she forgot the staring eyes, and let the moment take her, the music flowing through her in a heated rush, filling all the lonely spaces inside her, and flooding every dark, shadowy corner with light. The cobwebs that had gathered there over the past six years fluttered away, the thin, delicate threads vanishing into the air as he spun her from one turn into the next, his gaze holding hers, and his hand warm and firm against her back.

It was over too soon, just as all the sweetest moments were, the dream slipping from her grasp like water falling in silvery drops from her fingertips.

She came back to herself as the couples near them shifted, the rumble of the voices in the ballroom rising as the last note of the music faded.

But for one fleeting moment, neither of them moved.

In that instant, as they stood facing each other, time seemed to go still.

And it was strange... so strange, that the one thing she wanted the most in the world then was to lay her cheek against his chest, close her eyes, and hold onto it forever.

CHAPTER

FIFTEEN

"**M**ay I assist you, Lord Fairmont?"

James turned away from the window, startled. "Where did you come from, Crosby?"

"The hallway, my lord."

"Ah." He'd been a thousand miles away and hadn't noticed his bedchamber door opening. How long had he been standing here, staring out into his aunt's dark rose gardens? "What is it, Crosby?"

Crosby blinked. "Does your lordship wish for my assistance in undressing this evening?"

"Oh, right. That. No, thank you." James waved a hand toward the door and turned back to the window. "You may go."

"Very good, Lord Fairmont."

There was a shuffle of footsteps as Crosby crossed the bedchamber, and a moment later, the door closed.

Well, then. Now what?

It was a foolish question. Now he'd go to bed, of course. What else?

He tugged on the end of his cravat, unwound the

perfect Cascade knot Crosby had tied earlier, and tossed the length of silk onto the chair beside the bed, then stripped off his coat and waistcoat, and dropped them on top of his cravat.

It was late, well past time he went to his bed, yet as he unfastened his shirt cuffs, he found himself wandering back to the window, and gazing unseeing into the impenetrable darkness.

He was out of sorts, his head all muddled.

The house was silent around him, even the servants having taken to their beds. He should do the same, but a strange hesitancy was upon him as if he were waiting for something.

Only he didn't know what.

He closed his eyes, shutting out the pale glow of moonlight outside his window, but the velvet darkness had no time to settle over his eyelids before a picture arose, hazy at first, but becoming clearer with every breath he pulled into his lungs.

Miss Templeton, in her blue ball gown.

No, not Miss Templeton, but Euphemia. She'd never invited him to call her that, but when he thought of her now, he thought of her as Euphemia.

Not Phee. Somehow, the shortened version of her name didn't encompass all she was.

Not to him.

That gown she'd worn tonight... he'd never seen that shade of blue before.

Azure, his aunt had called it. Azure blue, a shade somewhere between sky blue, and cerulean. She was stunning in it, like a patch of the morning sky had been plucked from the heavens and set free in the middle of Lady Upton's ballroom.

No lady had ever worn a gown the way Euphemia had worn that gown this evening.

As if she had every right to it. As if it had been made only for her.

She'd come alive tonight, like a gorgeous, colorful butterfly bursting from its cocoon with a vengeance, and it... dear God, it was the most beautiful thing he'd ever seen.

The *ton* had been stunned silent. No doubt they were all still gossiping about timid Euphemia Templeton and her vivid blue gown, but Euphemia wasn't at all the fearful lady they all believed her to be.

She never had been.

She wasn't the lady he'd once believed her to be, either.

How had he ever thought her meek? How could she ever have thought herself a coward? He'd never met anyone braver than she was.

Tonight, she'd shown them all. He'd never been as proud to lead a lady to the dance floor as he had been tonight.

There'd been a few whispers and glares, yes— the *ton* was the *ton*, after all —and some of the same mocking laughter that had so upset her before, but this time, she hadn't run from it. She'd held her head high as she'd braved the people who'd tried to make her feel small, to make her cower.

She'd faced them all, and she'd danced.

As soon as he'd taken her into his arms, all the whispers had faded to silence, and all the staring eyes had vanished. It had been just the two of them then, whirling around the dance floor, her hand on his shoulder and his arm around her waist.

And now... he opened his eyes and glanced around his empty bedchamber.

What did he do with himself *now*? What did a man do, after such a dance as that? What became of a man, after he'd held such a lady in his arms? After he'd felt her every breath as if it were his own? He could feel her even now, as if she were still clasped in his arms, her skin warming him through the silk of his gloves.

He was in love with Euphemia Templeton.

He shook his head, a short laugh tearing loose from his throat. It was madness. Pure madness, but when had love ever made any sense?

As little as a few short weeks ago, he'd thought she was someone else, but it didn't matter. None of that mattered, because somehow, in just those few short weeks, he'd become *hers*.

Whether she'd become *his*... well, that was something else.

He braced his hands on the windowsill, his forehead against the glass, but there were no answers for him in the darkened gardens below.

Only shadows.

He didn't deserve her, but when she'd gazed at him tonight as they'd danced together, there'd been something in her eyes, something that made his heart surge with hope.

There was nothing to be done about it tonight, however. Tomorrow, he'd speak to her, tell her he was hers now, heart and soul, and beg her to be his in return.

But tomorrow was hours away yet, an eternity—

Tap, tap, tap.

He jerked upright, turning toward the door.

Someone was knocking, at this hour?

He took a hesitant step away from the window, his heart pounding, but no, it couldn't be. It was too much to hope for. No, it was likely just Crosby, come to collect his evening clothes in one of his fits of organization.

Tap, tap, tap.

He crossed the room, his heart in his throat, grasped the knob in his hand, and slowly, without daring to hope, he opened the door.

It wasn't Crosby.

Euphemia stood there, half lost in the shadows. "I beg your pardon, Lord Fairmont, but I forgot to... I couldn't fall asleep until I-I need to say something to you."

He stood there, mute. The azure gown was gone. She was wearing only a white night rail, the thin cotton billowing around her calves, her feet bare.

He blinked, terrified he'd conjured her from his fevered imagination, and she'd disappear, but she didn't. Instead, she inched closer, her long, dark eyelashes hiding her blue eyes.

"May I come in?"

There were a dozen reasons why he should turn her away at once. A thousand reasons she shouldn't enter his bedchamber, but not a single one could stop him from reaching for her.

He took her hand and drew her over the threshold.

She closed the door behind her, and leaned back against it, her gaze holding his.

And he... God, he wanted to wrap his arms around her waist and rest his cheek against her belly, but he didn't dare touch her, because if he did, he wouldn't be able to let her go.

So, he simply waited, his hands dangling awkwardly at his sides, and after a long silence, she took a step toward him— one, then another, until she was so close he could see the frantic flutter of her pulse in the hollow of her throat.

"I never thanked you for the dance tonight, my lord." She stepped closer, her hand coming up to cradle his cheek. "I've come to thank you now."

He didn't move— he couldn't have, even if he'd wanted to. He could do nothing but wait as she rose to her tiptoes and brought her lips to his.

YES. This was what he wanted. Her mouth, her shuddering breaths warm against his lips, her body pressed against his as she kissed him with a passion that swept everything before it, leaving only her.

He needed to taste her, would die if he didn't taste her.

"Euphemia." He teased the tip of his tongue against the seam of her lips, and she opened to him at once, her mouth wet and needy. She was so sweet, so perfect, but he'd had only a fleeting taste of her desire before she drew back.

"I've never... I don't know how to... I've never—"

"I know, sweetheart." He traced her jaw, catching his breath at the soft glide of her skin under his fingertips. "We should stop, but first, I..." How could he put into words what he wanted to say? His head was spinning, his heart a frenzied, wild thing in his chest.

Never had his heart beat as wildly as it did now, for *her*.

"I would never hurt you, Euphemia. Not for the world." It wasn't what he'd meant to say, but the words had tumbled from his lips before he knew he'd thought them, as if they'd been torn from his very soul.

She gazed up at him, her eyes two wide pools of dark, endless blue.

A shared breath passed between them, then another, and then she raised her arms, twined them around his neck, and melted against him. "Show me, James."

A low, pained groan left his lips.

He wanted to take her apart, to see inside her, touch every part of her with his hands and his mouth until he'd uncovered her every secret, revealed every part of her. He wanted to hold her in his arms, kiss those beautiful pink lips again and again, caress her soft, pale skin, and memorize the dozens of different shades of blue in her eyes.

But when he kissed her, it was soft, tentative— a question, rather than a demand. He traced his tongue over her lips, playing and teasing until the tension drained from her body. "Open your mouth for me, Euphemia."

She sighed as he dropped a tiny kiss onto one corner of her mouth. It was a small sound, the gentlest puff of air against his lips before she sank her hands into his hair and dragged him closer, her mouth parting under his.

"Yes, love. Please." He didn't know what he was begging for. He knew only that his entire body leaped to aching awareness as he surged inside, and, oh God, her mouth was so hot and sweet against his, and he was kissing her as if his life depended on the breath in her lungs, and his heart could only beat in time with hers.

"*James.*" She stroked her warm fingers over his neck, then slid them down to his chest. His stomach muscles tightened as her hands drifted lower, over his abdomen and under the hem of his shirt before coming to rest on the bare skin of his waist, her fingers leaving a trail of fire in their wake.

Too much...

He wanted her too much. Her sweet caresses were driving him to the edge of his control, but she was innocent, and he'd been telling the truth when he'd said he wouldn't hurt her for the world.

He caught her hands in his and drew them gently away from him. "Wait, Euphemia. We can't—"

"Please, James. Please don't send me away. I... I want to stay here with you tonight."

He caught her to him with a helpless groan, his every gentlemanly instinct abandoning him in the face of her soft pleading. "Come here, love," he whispered, wrapping his hands around her waist.

He stumbled backward toward his bed and dropped down onto it, pulling her into his lap. "So sweet, Phee. So soft and beautiful," he murmured as he slid one hand under her skirt to caress the impossibly soft skin on the inside of her knee.

"Oh, that tickles." She let out a soft laugh and buried her face in his neck.

"Hmmm. Is this better?" He traced his fingertips over the silky skin of her thigh, angling his head to trail his lips down her neck.

She shivered against him, and brought his mouth

back to hers with a firm tug on his hair that made his cock leap against her soft curves.

She made a low, needy sound in her throat and opened her mouth under his, chasing his tongue, coaxing it into her mouth, and, God above, she was stroking her tongue against his, her shyness falling away as she wriggled closer, her backside dragging over his throbbing cock, and it was too much, too good, and he was one moment away from clamping his hands down on her hips and rolling her beneath him.

Instead, he tore away from her with a groan and deposited her on his bed before jumping up and crossing to the other side of his bedchamber, far enough away from her that he couldn't snatch her back into his arms again.

"James?" She sat up, tugging her skirt down over her legs.

He didn't answer, only gazed at her, his breath coming in ragged pants.

She bit her lip. "Should I not have... did I do something wrong?"

"No! God, no. I was, er..." How to put this? "On the verge of forgetting I'm a gentleman." Even now he couldn't quite make his cock understand that he couldn't tumble her backward onto his bed, and lose himself in her sweet, soft body.

"I don't want you to be a gentleman. I may be innocent, James, but there can only be one reason for a lady to appear at a gentleman's bedchamber door alone, at night." For a moment, she looked uncertain. "You do know the reason, don't you?"

He choked out a laugh. Dear God, she was irresistible. "I have some idea, yes."

"Then you know that I..." She looked down at her hands, a blush tingeing her cheeks.

He drew closer, and caught her chin in his fingers, raising her face to his. "Do you want me, Euphemia?"

He expected more blushes, perhaps a bit of maidenly stammering, but she met his gaze and held it. "Yes."

"Why..." He cleared his throat. "Why me? Because I taught you to waltz?"

Because that wasn't enough, not nearly enough for him to have earned the gift of her.

"No." She let out a long, slow breath. "Because you *see* me, James, and no one... no one else ever has before."

He stilled for an instant, but it was hopeless, trying to resist her. His heart wouldn't allow him to send her away.

So, he gathered her into his arms, because there was nothing else he *could* do, and because it was true, what she'd said.

He *did* see her.

All her sweetness, all the love she held inside her, all the secrets she'd kept hidden for so many years... he saw all of it. All of her, everything she was, and to see her was to love her with everything inside of him, and everything *he* was.

Nothing could have torn him from her arms then, but he wouldn't take her.

Not until she was his.

But he could give her pleasure, and then he could wrap her in his arms, and hold her until the sun rose. He gathered her close, and eased her back against the bed. "Lie down, sweetheart."

She did so, settling back against the pillows, and

gazing up at him with huge, trusting eyes. "Come here, James."

She opened her arms to him, and something shifted inside his chest, then. Something small but vital that would never shift back again.

He'd never again be the man he once was, before her.

He held her for a long time, stroking her soft skin and whispering to her, trying to put into words how she'd changed him, made him a better man than he'd been, but he felt too much at once, and the words tangled in his mouth.

So, he kissed her with all the love he felt for her and prayed she understood what he didn't know how to say. He kissed her and kissed her until the passion between them sparked into a conflagration.

She was panting, fistfuls of his shirt clutched in her hands. "James?"

He kissed her throat, the curve of her jaw, and the soft skin behind her ear. "Yes, love?"

She tugged at the linen. "Take this off."

He dropped a hot, open-mouthed kiss between her breasts before he drew back, and tugged his shirt over his head.

"Oh my," she breathed, reaching a hesitant hand out to trace the lines of his stomach, her eyes widening as his muscles shifted under her touch. "Is that alright?"

He let out a soft laugh as he stretched out beside her on the bed. "Yes." He caught her hand, and pressed it against the center of his chest, over his heart. "I want your hands on me."

She gave him a shy smile as she caressed her palm over his chest. He sucked in a breath when her fingertip grazed his nipple, and she froze. "Oh! I shouldn't have—"

"Don't stop. It feels so good, sweetheart."

She did it again, dragging her fingertip lightly over his nipple, her gaze darting to his face when he let out a groan. A wondering smile curved her lips. "You seem to like that."

Teasing minx. "I do like it. Shall I show you why?"

She nodded, and he slid his hand into the loose neck of her night rail, easing it off her shoulder and baring one of her breasts to him. "So pretty, Euphemia," he breathed, stroking his thumb over one of the sweet pink peaks.

"Oh!" Her back arched at the caress. "That's so..."

"It feels good, doesn't it?" He touched her again, teasing her nipples with gentle strokes of his thumbs, and God, it was heady, her innocent surprise as he coaxed her body to arousal with slow, gentle caresses, until soft whimpers and pleas were falling from her lips.

He drew back, taking in her pale, delicate skin, her pink cheeks, the dark silk of her hair spread out across his pillow, and her eyes, such a deep, endless blue.

He'd fallen in love with her eyes weeks ago, hadn't he?

"God, look at you. You're so beautiful, Euphemia. I want to taste you. Here." He leaned closer, teasing his lips over the tip of her breast, suckling and nipping at her until she was writhing against him, her nipples flushed a deep, cherry red. "And here." He caught the hem of her night rail and drew it slowly up her thighs, pausing to caress the silky skin there before brushing his fingers over the tangle of curls between her legs. "And here." He parted her damp folds and stroked his fingertip gently over her tender bud.

Her gaze jerked to his face, her cheeks going scarlet. "I'm not sure that's..."

Whatever protest she'd been about to offer trailed off into an incoherent moan as he touched her, circling her sweet bud until she was panting, and her hips began to move in time with his caresses.

He teased and stroked her until she was arching beneath him, then he slid down her body, dropping kisses as he went, his breath coming in harsh pants until at last— *at last* —he nudged his head between her legs, and touched the tip on his tongue to her core.

"James!" She jerked underneath him, her hands sinking into his hair, her fingers gripping hard.

God, he'd waited a lifetime for this, hadn't he? For *her*, mindless with desire beneath him, unable to think of anything but the pleasure he was giving her.

He groaned against her warm folds, holding her open to him with a hand on each of her trembling thighs as he teased her with light caresses of his lips and tongue, but her soft whimpers were driving him mad, and he soon abandoned his teasing and stroked his tongue over her again and again, until she went rigid beneath him.

"James!" Her bud swelled against his tongue as the pleasure swept over her, tearing a breathless moan from her lips. He stayed with her, wringing every last shudder from her until at last she subsided, her limbs going limp. He crawled back up the bed then, and drew her into his arms, ignoring his throbbing cock as he stroked her hair and murmured to her, telling her how sweet she was, how beautiful.

She was quiet for a few moments, flushed and dazed, but when her breathing quieted, she turned in his arms, facing him. "That was... I'm not sure what to say."

He reached out to toy with a lock of her hair, chuckling. "Miss Euphemia Templeton, struck speechless? I never thought I'd see the day."

"Me, either."

She brushed his hair back from his face in a gesture so tender it made his throat ache. She cradled his cheek in her hand for a moment before sliding it down his neck to his chest, then to his lower belly, sifting her fingers through the trail of dark hair that began under his navel, and disappeared under the waistband of his pantaloons.

His cock, already hard and straining for her gave a hopeful twitch as her hand drew closer to it. A groan fell from his lips, and her hand froze, her breath catching. "May I touch you now?"

Touch him? Good Lord, even the thought of her small, dainty hand on his cock made him so wild he was in danger of disgracing himself. Just her gaze on his straining length was enough to tear another tortured moan from his lips. "I'm not sure that's... ah."

She touched him then— just the softest caress with one fingertip, more an experiment than anything else, but it was enough to silence every protest in his head.

All he could think about was her touching him, stroking him...

She loosened one of the buttons of his falls, then the other. He let out another desperate moan, his neck arching as she lowered his falls. His swollen cock sprang free, and without any hesitation, she wrapped her small, warm hand around him.

"Oh," she murmured, tightening her fingers around his aching erection. "Your skin is so soft here."

"Is it?" Nothing about his cock felt soft to him at the moment, but he let out a strained laugh and did his best not to push into her hand.

"Is this how I'm meant to do it?" She gave him an experimental caress. "Show me, James. I want..."

She trailed off, and he jerked his gaze to her face. She was gazing down at his hard length cradled in her palm, her brows drawn together. "Yes? What do you want, love?"

"I want to give you pleasure, as you did me, but I'm not sure... I don't want to hurt you." She flushed, but bravely met his eyes. "Will you show me how to touch you?"

There was only one proper response to such a question, and that was to refuse her, and tuck himself back into his pantaloons this instant. A gentleman didn't permit an innocent lady to bring him to climax, but she was so sweet, her eyes so big and blue as she gazed up at him, and he wanted her so badly....

"Hold me a little tighter, love, and... yes, that's it. Now stroke me, like this." He laid his hand over hers, and moved her hand up his hard length, then down again.

She wrapped her fingers more firmly around him, and gave him a long, steady stroke. "Like this? Is this alright?"

Yes," he hissed. "So good, Euphemia. So perfect."

There was no holding back, after that. His hips were moving, jerking in time to each stroke of her hand, and God, he was so close, his spine tingling, and his lower belly going tight...

"Ah, God. Yes, sweetheart. Don't stop, don't—"

He shot into her hand, his back bowing with pleasure. She gasped softly, but she stroked him through his climax, until he fell back against the bed, still shuddering from the intensity of his release.

They lay quietly afterward, her head cradled on his chest, until her breaths grew deep and even, and her heavy eyelids slid closed.

He didn't fall asleep at once. He held her against him, stroking her dark hair and watching the glow of the moonlight peeking through the draperies caress her face.

At some point, he must have fallen asleep.

He woke the next morning to sunlight streaming through the window, and an empty bed.

Euphemia was gone.

CHAPTER

SIXTEEN

OXFORDSHIRE, ENGLAND, TWO DAYS
LATER

The rain started just after James passed through Bletchingdon. It wasn't a gentle, warm spring rain, but a chilling downpour that sneaked under the neckline of his coat in a relentless drizzle.

By the time he arrived at Steeple Cross, he was soaked to the skin. If that hadn't been enough to persuade him he was being punished for making such a mess of things with Euphemia, the welcome he received when he arrived at Steeple Cross certainly was.

He was halfway up the long, winding drive when the front door opened, and four gentlemen stepped out. Not the usual sort of gentlemen, but four tall, broad-shouldered, unsmiling gentlemen, their thick arms crossed over their chests.

He knew who they were, of course.

The *ton* might delight in heaping scorn on the Templeton sisters' heads, but even the most spiteful gossips didn't dare breathe a word against them within hearing distance of their husbands who— if the rumors were true —could turn savage in defense of their wives.

ANNA BRADLEY

He'd expected Cross would be here, of course. It was his estate. But Melrose, and Chatham, too? Then there was Prestwick, who had reason enough to dislike him, even putting aside the mistakes he'd made with Euphemia.

Two days ago, he'd taken an innocent lady to his bed, only to wake the next morning to find she hadn't only fled his bedchamber, but London itself!

Or, well... she hadn't *fled*, precisely. Her family had sent for her to come to Steeple Cross to help her sister Juliet through a difficult lying-in. She'd left Fosberry House early the morning after their night together before he'd had a chance to say a word to her.

She was gone before he'd told her he loved her or made her a single promise. She'd left without a word of affection from him, not a word of reassurance regarding their future together. He should have spilled his heart to her, the night he'd held her in his arms.

Instead, he'd failed her.

So, he'd come to grovel, and it looked as if he'd have to start here.

He reined in his horse, removed his hat, and wiped the raindrops from his forehead, eyeing the four men who stood between him and the front door.

God above. He'd be lucky to get a single toe over the threshold.

But he'd come here prepared to claim the lady he loved, and if he had to get past them to get to her, then so be it.

He nudged his horse into a walk and approached the front door.

Prestwick was the first to step forward. "Fairmont."

"Prestwick."

He and Prestwick had been friends once before James had ruined it by accusing Prestwick of having nefarious designs on Harriett—an accusation that had proved utterly unfounded. He'd apologized, but judging by Prestwick's unfriendly expression, the man hadn't forgiven him.

Prestwick took in his soaked coat and dripping hat. "It's a pity you've come all this way only to have to turn back again."

James straightened in the saddle. "I'm not going anywhere, Prestwick."

Lord Cross let out a huff. "This is my *home*, Fairmont, and you're not welcome here."

Evidently not, but he didn't give a damn. "I'm not going anywhere until I speak to Euphemia."

Lord Melrose raised an eyebrow. "I believe you mean *Miss Templeton*."

Well, that was plain enough, but if they thought he'd turn around and run back off to London, they'd be disappointed.

There was no turning around, and no going back now. Euphemia was *his*, and he *would* see her, even if he had to ride his horse through the front door and directly into Cross's entryway. "No, Melrose. I don't believe I did."

Lord Chatham, a tall, dark-haired man with a forbidding countenance moved to stand behind Prestwick. "Look, Fairmont, I don't know what happened between you and Miss Templeton, but—"

"What *did* happen between you?" Prestwick demanded. "I know something bloody well did, because she's been downcast since she arrived, and—"

"And we think you're to blame for it," Melrose interrupted. "Comport yourself as a gentleman should, Fairmont, and be on your way. Unless, of course, you fancy a brawl right here on Cross's front steps."

James glanced from one unfriendly face to the next, before finally settling on Prestwick. If he spoke from his heart, perhaps his old friend would hear him. "I've made mistakes with Euphemia, but I love her, Kit. Surely, that's all that matters?"

Prestwick's eyebrows shot up. "You're in *love* with Phee?"

"Madly in love, yes. If I loved her less, perhaps I wouldn't have made such a mess of it, but can you honestly say you didn't make mistakes with Mathilda when you fell in love with her?" James glanced from one man to the next. "Can any of you?"

The men shuffled their feet, avoiding each other's eyes until a sly smile curved Cross's lips. "When Chatham here fell in love with Helena, he tried to dismiss her as his governess, and threatened to throw her out of his house."

"For God's sake, Cross!" Chatham glowered at him. "That was meant to be private, and anyway, you're no better. You told Juliet she wasn't welcome at your house party, and ordered her gone, and this after she'd just been in a carriage accident!"

"Damn it, Chatham—"

Cross was interrupted by a burst of laughter from Melrose. "Prestwick's idea of a proper courtship was to ask Tilly to matchmake him with another lady."

"And you, Melrose, got sotted, kissed a lady in a darkened library, and the next day you couldn't remember who she was." Cross gave Melrose an evil grin. "Not very becoming of the Nonesuch, eh?"

James stared at them. Oh, this was much better

than he'd dared hope. "Are you saying, gentlemen, that all of you made as much of a mess of your courtships as I did?"

"Of course, we did." Kit rolled his eyes. "Gentlemen always make a mess of the courtship."

"There's nothing in the world as ridiculous as a man in love." Melrose wiped the tears of laughter from his eyes. "It's a miracle any of us won over our wives. Gentlemen, we don't deserve them."

"No, and Fairmont here doesn't deserve Phee, but I don't suppose he's any less deserving than any of us. God knows he looks miserable enough." Chatham waved a hand at James's shivering, dripping form. "Just as a man desperately in love ought to look. I say we let him speak to her."

"THERE'S some sort of standoff taking place outside," Tilly announced from the window seat, her gaze fixed on the drive below.

Phee, who'd hardly taken her eyes off her newborn niece since the baby had first been placed in her arms a day ago paid no mind to this but turned to Juliet with a smile. "She has the most perfect face, does she not? Her mouth looks just like a tiny rosebud."

"It does." Juliet reached out to stroke her daughter's hand. "I think she's going to have Miles's eyes."

"Standoff?" Emmeline had been fussing over Juliet's pillows, but now she turned to Tilly with a frown. "What sort of standoff?"

"I can't say, exactly." Tilly pressed closer to the glass to get a better look. "But Kit, Johnathan, Miles, and Adrian are all down there, menacing some poor gentleman who's arrived on horseback."

"What, all four of them? No good will come of that." Helena hurried to the window and peered over Tilly's shoulder. "Who is that gentleman? I don't recognize him."

"It's difficult to tell, half-drowned as he is, but it looks rather like..." Tilly broke off with a gasp. "It *is*! It's Lord Fairmont!"

"Lord Fairmont!" Phee jumped up, the baby clutched in her arms, her legs suddenly as wobbly as a jelly beneath her. "James is *here*?"

"James, is it?" Tilly arched an eyebrow, a knowing smile on her lips. "I *knew* something had happened! Why, I saw it as soon as you arrived, Phee! Didn't I say so, Helena?"

"You did, but I confess I thought your imagination had run away with you. Now, however..." Helena turned to Phee, her eyes wide. "Is there something you wish to confide in us, Phee?"

Confide in them? Confide *what*? That three nights ago she'd shamelessly presented herself at Lord Fairmont's bedchamber door? That he'd taken her to his bed, and he'd... and she'd... goodness, she couldn't even think of it without a blush. Or should she confess that only hours later, she'd run away from him, without a word of warning or explanation?

She was the most disgraceful coward.

But she'd never asked for anything from James, and neither did she expect anything. She hadn't gone to his bedchamber hoping he'd make promises of eternal love and devotion. She'd gone because, for just one night, she'd wanted to lie in the arms of the man she loved.

Tilly jumped up from the window seat, rushed over to Phee, and plucked the baby from her arms. "Quickly, Phee! Go and change your dress. Baby Euphemia drooled on that one. Wear your blue one, mind, and not that dreadful brown!"

"Me? Why should I change? Lord Fairmont hasn't come here for *me*."

"Of course, he's come for you!" Tilly threw her hands up in the air. "Why else would he have come?"

"He looks as if he's ready to do battle for you too, Phee. Oh, wait. They're laughing now, and it looks like... yes, they're letting him in." Helena turned away from the window, hurried across the room to Phee, and began tugging her toward the door. "Go down at once."

"But the drool!" Phee glanced down at her gown in despair.

"Never mind the drool." Emmeline jerked open the door, and pushed her out into the hallway. "Gentlemen don't notice that sort of thing."

"Especially gentlemen in love! Oh, and Phee, don't forget to—"

Emmeline closed the door, cutting Tilly off, and leaving Phee alone in the hallway.

Slowly, she made her way to the staircase, her heart beating wildly in her chest.

Had James come here for *her*? It seemed impossible, yet she couldn't think of any other reason he'd come to Steeple Cross. Was he angry with her for leaving Fosberry House so abruptly? She'd considered slipping a note under his door but in the end...

In the end, she'd gone away without a word, because...

Because she'd been afraid. Afraid he'd regret what

they'd done, and that she'd be able to see it in his face the following morning. Afraid of the depths of her feelings for him, and afraid he'd never return them.

"Euphemia."

She stilled.

He was standing alone in the entryway below, his hat in his hands, rain dripping from the hem of his cloak.

"James," she whispered. It had only been a few days, but how she'd missed him!

"Come here, Euphemia." He held out his hand to her.

And she... well, what else could she do but come down the last few steps, and take it? What more could she want than to feel his strong, warm fingers clasp her own?

Nothing. There wasn't a single thing she wanted more than that.

Than *him*.

He led her down the corridor to the drawing room and closed the door behind them. For a moment they both stood there, staring silently at each other until he cleared his throat. "Three nights ago, you came to my bedchamber, Euphemia. Why?"

He didn't know? Had he not read the truth in her every whisper, her every touch?

When she didn't answer at once, he shook his head. "You told me it wasn't because I taught you to waltz, but—"

"It wasn't." She couldn't bear to let him think so. Not when her feelings were so much stronger, so much more tender than mere gratitude. "I swear it to you, James."

"Why, then?"

"Because I…" She might have let her fear take over then, but love, it seemed, would have its way, because the words were already rushing from her heart into her mouth, and falling off the edge of her tongue. "Because I wanted you, James, and because I…"

He drew closer. "You?"

"I-I love you," she whispered.

But it wouldn't do, that timid whisper. When you told a man you loved him, you did it with your entire voice, and with everything inside you. She drew closer, pressed her palm to his cheek, and looked into his eyes. "I love you, James."

His face changed in an instant, the tension in his jaw releasing, and the boyish smile she loved so well — the lopsided one that made his eyes twinkle —lit up his face.

She'd only ever seen that smile when he looked at *her*.

"And why do you suppose I took you to my bed, Euphemia?"

She swallowed, and shook her head.

"Because I wanted you, too, you maddening woman! I *still* want you. I want you forever, Euphemia. I'm in love with you." He gazed down at her with soft eyes. "Did you truly believe I'd let you go?"

She had believed it. At least, the dark corner inside her where all her old fears still lived had believed it, but that voice had grown quieter since she'd found James.

Perhaps the time had come to silence it entirely.

Love, after all, was so much stronger than fear.

"Don't you see, Euphemia?" He stroked a fingertip down her cheek. "You're mine now, and I'm yours. I've been yours for weeks, I think."

The look in his eyes as he gazed down at her was so loving, so tender that hot tears rushed to her eyes. "I didn't know."

He let out a soft laugh. "Nor did I, at first. I've never been in love before, you see."

She peeked up at him from under her lashes. "Me, either."

He drew her into his arms then and buried his face in her hair. "You're trembling."

"Yes." But there was no fear inside her. Only love.

She tucked herself against him and laid her cheek against his chest. "Your heart is beating so quickly."

"In time with yours, Euphemia," he murmured against her hair. "It beats in time with yours."

EPILOGUE

"Behold your future, Lady Fairmont."

Phee had been turning over the first leaves of her latest Gothic horror novel— a wonderfully spine-chilling tome entitled *Frankenstein* —but she looked up, following James's glance.

Lord Cross was seated in a leather chair tucked into the opposite corner of the drawing room, and baby Euphemia— or Mimi, as she was called, to distinguish her from her namesake —was enthroned upon his knee, giggling in delight, handfuls of his dark hair caught in her chubby fists.

"As Miles is Mimi's papa, I'd sooner call that *your* future, my lord. Mine looks a great deal more peaceful." She nodded toward Juliet, who was perched on the arm of the chair, her hand on her husband's shoulder, and a sweet smile on her lips.

"Very well then, if you insist upon splitting hairs, it's *our* future, and a more worrying one I can't imagine." He gave a despairing shake of his head, but for all his grumbling, he couldn't hide the naked yearning on his face as he watched Miles bouncing Mimi on his knee.

Phee set her book aside and slipped her hand into his, her heart swelling with warmth. "They are enamored of her, aren't they?"

She'd never seen Juliet so happy, and Miles... well, he'd never been one to wear his emotions on his face, but there was no mistaking the tenderness in his dark eyes when he gazed at Juliet and their daughter.

"Enamored? Is that what you'd call it? It looks more like madness to me." James sniffed, but a smile was twitching at the corners of his lips. "Just look at them. She's going to snatch him bald."

"He doesn't seem to mind."

"No, and that's precisely my point. She's plucking him like a chicken, and he's laughing. *Laughing*!"

"Yes? What is your objection, my lord? Wait, I think I know." She reached up and gave one of his dark curls a playful tug. "I shouldn't worry. You have plenty to spare."

"It's the point of the thing. Cross was infamous at Oxford for being a disagreeable sort of gentleman but just look at him now. A perfectly good irascible earl, brought low by a tiny little bit of a human with drool running down her chin."

"Do you intend to be a stern papa then, James?" She laid a tender hand on the slight swell of her belly. "Will you frown upon giggling, and forbid drooling?"

"God, no. I daresay our child will run roughshod over the both of us, and we'll find it utterly charming. Daughters are the worst, you know. They wrap their poor papas around their tiny fingers."

"Yes, and that's just as it should be." Her father had been a doting papa, hopelessly enthralled with his five daughters. He'd used to tell anyone who'd listen that they were the cleverest, kindest, and loveliest young ladies in England.

How she wished he were here to see them all now!

It was a lucky thing the drawing room at Steeple Barton was such a large one because a smaller one wouldn't have held them all. Everywhere she looked — from the settees gathered in front of the fire, to the overstuffed chairs scattered about, to the large games table that dominated a corner of the room —she found a Templeton.

They had spread and multiplied until they covered every surface.

Tilly, Helena, and Harriett were lounging on the settee, their heads together, laughing over some story Helena was telling about her twin boys, Adrian and Etienne, who were dreadfully mischievous, and forever getting into some scrape or other.

Emmeline, Johnathan, and Johnathan's three younger sisters had crowded into a window seat along with Kit, Gilly, and Adrian, and the eight of them were engaged in a rather noisy game of charades. Lady Fosberry had retired to an adjacent chair with baby Samuel in her arms, and was cooing nonsense at him, while he gazed up at her in wonder, his dark eyes wide.

There'd been a time, not so long ago when Phee had been certain her family wouldn't recover from the blows they'd been dealt— that they'd continue to wither away until the Templetons were nothing but a memory, the family name dying alongside them — but fate, bless her, had a different future in mind for them.

Somehow, they'd been granted grace, and fortune had smiled on them.

Instead of withering, they'd grown, adding new faces to their family with every year that passed.

Fate willing, they'd continue to do so.

She stroked her palm over her belly. Next year, there would be one more new face. Perhaps more than one. Time would tell.

"Will you have a boy, Lady Fairmont, or do you fancy a daughter first?" James covered her hand with his own, smiling down at her. "What's your preference?"

"I'd quite like a boy, one day." Didn't every lady with five sisters wish for a son? "If not this one, then the next. It doesn't matter."

"No, it doesn't." He pressed a gentle kiss to her temple. "As long as our children have blue eyes, then I'm content."

"I daresay you'll get that wish, as we both have blue eyes."

"No, they must be dark blue. Not my eyes, but *yours*, Euphemia."

Her breath caught at the slight tremor in his voice when he said her name, the warmth and love in his eyes when he gazed down at her, and... oh dear, her eyes were stinging, and she was certain her nose must be turning red.

She reached up and cupped his cheek in her palm. "I love you, James. More than words can say."

"No more than I love you." He caught her hand in his and brought her fingers to his lips. "You brought me back to life, Euphemia."

"James," Lady Fosberry called. "What are you

saying to Euphemia that has her looking as if she's about to burst into a flood of tears?"

"And as red as a peony, too," Tilly added, with a sly grin.

"Oh, do leave poor Phee alone." Juliet rose from her chair with a brisk clap of her hands. "Come, it's growing dark. If we're to have our walk, we'd best go now."

"Is it so late as that?" Phee glanced toward the window.

Twilight was descending, wrapping the sky in deep violet. A pink glow was still visible in the west, but it was fading quickly, so they scurried about, fetching their warmest cloaks and hats to ward off the December chill, and then the whole party set off outdoors.

"I don't know how anyone can prefer London to the country." Emmeline let out a contented sigh as they all made their way down a crushed gravel path toward a pretty little garden at the southern corner of the grounds. "You can't see the stars, for all the dirt and grime there."

"My darling wife, the *ton* would be horrified to hear you say so." Johnathan drew her closer against his side. "Don't you know London is the center of the world?"

"I certainly don't miss it," Adrian said, catching Helena's hand. "Do you, Prestwick?"

"God, no." He cast a fond look at Tilly. "I have everything I need right here."

"Perhaps you miss the matchmaking, Phee?" Harriett's eyes were bright with laughter as came up alongside Phee, Gilly's hand in hers.

"No, indeed. My matchmaking days are over, but I

can't deny some truly magical things came of it." She squeezed James's hand. "Some wonderful, magical things."

"They did, indeed. Whoever would have thought we'd all end up here?" Juliet gazed up at the stars twinkling to life in the sky above them. "The disgraced Templeton sisters, whose wishes all came true."

"Why, I did." A secret smile curved Lady Fosberry's lips. "I knew it all along."

214

ALSO BY ANNA BRADLEY

Tainted Angels

Boughs of Folly

Then in a Twinkling

Games Earls Play

Not Just Any Earl

Odd Earl Out

Fell in Love with an Earl

Earl Crazy

Here Comes My Earl

Drop Dead Dukes

Give the Devil His Duke

Damned if I Duke

The Swooning Virgins Society

The Virgin who Ruined Lord Gray

The Virgin who Vindicated Lord Darlington

The Virgin Who Humbled Lord Haslemere

The Virgin Who Bewitched Lord Lymington

The Virgin Who Captured a Viscount

The Sutherland Sisters

Lady Eleanor's Seventh Suitor

Lady Charlotte's First Love

Twelfth Night with the Earl

The Sutherland Scandals

A Wicked Way to Win an Earl

A Season of Ruin

The Somerset Sisters

More or Less a Marchioness

More or Less a Countess

More or Less a Temptress

Besotted Scots

The Wayward Bride

To Wed a Wild Scot

For the Sake of a Scottish Rake

The Witching Hour

ABOUT THE AUTHOR

Anna Bradley writes steamy, sexy Regency historical romance—think garters, fops and riding crops! Readers can get in touch with Anna via her webpage at http://www.annabradley.net. Anna lives with her husband and two children in Portland, OR, where people are delightfully weird and love to read.

Printed in the USA
CPSIA information can be obtained
at www.ICGtesting.com
LVHW030449120424
777132LV00014B/288

9 781648 395895